A Sparrow Alone

BY ALICIA PETERSEN

journeyforth®

Greenville, South Carolina

Library of Congress Cataloging-in-Publication Data
Petersen, Alicia, date.
  A sparrow alone / by Alicia Petersen.
    p. cm.
  Summary: Saddened by the death of her parents at the hands of soldiers in
Roman-occupied Jerusalem, Mala, a seventeen-year-old Jewish seamstress,
finds no comfort from her older brother Abdon, who is consumed with
anger, until they each meet Jesus of Nazareth.
  ISBN 1-59166-204-4 (Perfect bound paperback : alk. paper)
  [1. Brothers and sisters—Fiction. 2. Orphans—Fiction. 3. Jesus Christ—
Fiction. 4. Jews—History—168 B.C.-135 A.D.—Fiction.] I. Title.
  PZ7.P44187Sp 2004
  [Fic]—dc22

                                                              2003026624

Cover Photo Credit: TJ Getz

Visit bjupress.com to access a free discussion guide.

Design by Jamie Miller
Composition by Melissa Matos

©2004 by BJU Press
Greenville, South Carolina 29614
JourneyForth Books is a division of BJU Press

Printed in the United States of America

ISBN 978-1-59166-204-4

15 14 13 12 11 10 9 8 7 6 5 4 3 2

For my children—
earliest and best
hearers of my stories

Contents

CHAPTER 1

Bethphage lay quiet under the crescent moon's silent, arched passage of the heavens. Cobbled streets and dusty alleyways wove silver threads between the dark squares of houses. The entire village seemed asleep, man and beast alike at rest from their long day's toil. One window, however, revealed a flickering glow.

On a stool pulled close to the room's tiny charcoal brazier a young woman bent forward so that her work was lighted by the glowing coals as well as by the small clay lamp to her left. Mala's fingers moved mechanically about their familiar task with fabric, needle, and thread, but her mind chased itself about over well-worn, mazelike thought paths.

He was all she had. Each was, in fact, all the other had. And yet, it was enough. At least it had been. But now? Mala poked the embers of the dying fire, urging from it one final burst of warmth against the room's chill. Then she again drew close to the flickering oil lamp, blinking back tears. She had promised this garment—finished—to the Lady Terentia, her most influential Roman client. Mala sighed. Until a few moments ago she had been enjoying her work, exulting in the shimmering green silk upon the shoulder of which she was embroidering delicate flowers. But then thoughts of Abdon had shattered her peace.

Abdon. His face refused to leave her mind. How she loved him, her brother. He had been her world since their parents—innocent bystanders in a Jerusalem marketplace—had been trampled to death by mounted Roman soldiers quelling a riot. Brother and sister had been forced into instant independence. Just three months before their parents' death Abdon had proudly enjoyed the synagogue ceremony that signaled his manhood. Surely, he had reassured his little sister, Jehovah had thus prepared him for mature responsibility.

Aided only by a teacher in the synagogue, Abdon had supervised the funeral and burial of their parents. But nightmares plagued him from that time on, jolting him awake, tearful and trembling. Only Mala knew how she would race to her brother's sleeping mat, then talk to him gently, holding his hand, until he calmed and slept again.

So brother and sister had become a world unto themselves, refusing various neighbors' halfhearted offers of help. Their mutual bereavement and daily struggle to survive had bonded them strongly. The intervening years that had brought Mala to seventeen summers of life and Abdon to nineteen had been marked by their physical stamina and emotional determination. Recently, however, Abdon's behavior threatened not only their accomplishment, but also their relationship; he seemed increasingly alienated from her.

"Oh!" Mala cried out as she jabbed her needle in frustration at the fabric and instead drove its point into a finger. She stared at the tiny drop of blood oozing from her flesh. How it pictured the hurt of her heart! But she must keep the blood from marring Lady Terentia's garment . . .

"So . . . my sister has reverted to sucking on her finger like a child."

Mala whirled toward the door. "Abdon! How could I miss sounds of your return?"

"You were absorbed in nursing your finger, Sparrow. A merchantman's camel could have come stomping in without your notice." Abdon plopped cross-legged onto the floor close to the brazier's warmth. "Ah, but what of the luxurious garment for Our Lady Nose-in-the-Air?"

"Abdon, please. I enjoy handling these lovely fabrics and threads."

Abdon turned his face toward the dying charcoal; its glow emphasized the new hardness of his mouth. "Enjoy! Why must you only handle these things, Mala? You're more fit to keep them in your hands than is your arrogant Roman patroness!"

Letting the shimmering garment slip from her lap, Mala reached across to place her hand on Abdon's cheek. "Why do you speak with such anger, Abdon?"

"Show me reason for anything else: This place made bare by selling what we had that we might have what we need? Victuals scant for survival? You and I with bodies roughly clothed, hands roughly worked? Looks of disdain from the Romans, pity from our people? Aye, there's abundant cause for anger, Sister. Since you'll not acknowledge it, I've plenty for both of us."

"This isn't like you, Abdon. Yours has been the strength, the hope on which I've leaned these years since we've been alone."

"The strength of patience has betrayed us; hope's vision has proven a mirage. We've waited for a kindly fate, believed in a just God. No more. The waiting, the belief, are not only vain; they're marks of a fool. These hands will wrestle fate and turn his smile toward us. This mind will work its own will, providing those things withheld from us so long—"

"You speak against Jehovah God, my brother! You—who taught me the Psalmist's words, 'The Lord executeth righteousness and judgment for all that are oppressed.' "

"Words." Abdon fairly snarled his reply. "Words. That's all they are—empty words. There can be no more reliance upon vanity. Bid farewell to Abdon the Weak, Sister. And greet Abdon the Strong."

Mala could not prevent tears spilling from her eyes. "But in saying that, you renounce everything Mother and Father—"

"The filthy Romans took away our mother and our father. These years of their absence I've tried with all my heart to walk in our parents' precepts. The result? This." He swept his arms wide, indicating the cold, bare room. "Only a fool continues on a path that leads nowhere. I am no such fool." Abdon rose abruptly. "From this night on I walk a new pathway. And I walk it a new man." He bent to kiss Mala's tear-streaked cheek. "Your tears will soon be turned to smiles, Sparrow. You'll see." With that Abdon hurried out the door and back into the night.

As silence returned to the room, Mala felt the shaking of an awful doubt. Was Abdon right and she wrong? It did seem that their efforts had wrought little of worth. Each time she had been in one of the great city houses, she'd realized the chasm of difference that lay between the Roman woman's plenty and her own poverty. But no—she mustn't entertain such thoughts. She shook herself and blew on her fingers; she rubbed her hands together. But as the chill of her body lessened, that of her heart deepened. Who was this new Abdon? A stranger had replaced the gentle brother she adored.

Drying her tears, Mala retrieved the bright silk puddled on the floor and bent again to her sewing. She must bring her thoughts back to the present, to the work at hand. Her mind must not follow Abdon into the unknown darkness that lay beyond the doorway.

CHAPTER 2

Dawn streamed through the eastern window and across Mala's sleeping form, touching the rough blanket with color. The girl stretched, yearning to turn again to sleep after the night's scant rest. But she must be up, must deliver the finished garment to Lady Terentia. She left her bed, hurriedly straightened the blanket, dashed cold water from a clay ewer onto face and neck, and shivered into her tunic. She leaned from the window, noting the length of the morning shadows. She must hurry! She knew that early delivery of a garment on the promised day pleased Lady Terentia, made her less loathe to part with payment.

Mala shrugged into her aba, sorry that the chill morning made the coat necessary. Scrupulously clean, as was each item of her clothing, the aba nevertheless fairly screamed its age. Wrapping her veil about her head, Mala caught up the silk dress in one hand, a bit of parched corn in the other. Then she hurried into the dawn-laced street.

The village of Bethphage still lay mostly asleep. Only those, like her, who had early business in the city were about at this hour. Her sandals moved quickly over the familiar cobbles. She turned onto the dusty road outside the village just as she finished eating the final bit of corn.

"Mala! Ho—a slower pace might win you company for your journey . . ."

Mala stopped and turned. Tahath's familiar square form hurried toward her. He led a donkey dwarfed by the bundles it bore. The perpetual sadness of the animal's face contrasted with that of his smiling master. The girl felt some of her tension depart. Tahath always had that effect on her. Although he was the same age as Abdon, Tahath's cheerful practicality somehow lent him an air of greater maturity. Mala silently thanked Jehovah for sending her friend on this particular day. "Good morning, Tahath. I would welcome company into the city. Only necessity takes me there! Bethphage's quiet is much more to my liking."

"I know that, Mala. It has been so since our childhood." His voice took on a teasing note. "It seems to me that a considerate brother should make this trip for you."

"I . . . Abdon can't . . . he isn't . . ."

Tahath's expression sobered. "Forgive me, Mala. I didn't mean unkindness to either Abdon or you."

"I know. You're a true friend to both of us." Mala struggled over the decision to share or withhold her sisterly concerns. A quick glance at Tahath's strong profile against the lightening horizon quelled her reluctance. "Though I try not to be, I'm fearful for Abdon. He is . . . changed. Perhaps I'm foolish, but it frightens me."

"Foolish you've never been. May a friend know your concern?"

They were walking side by side now, the donkey's hooves whispering *pockety-pockety* behind them in the dust. Mala blinked back tears of gratitude. She knew that anything she told Tahath would be kept confidential. She also knew him to be wise beyond his years. "Abdon's . . . change . . . has not come suddenly. For months now he has talked less, . . . smiled less, . . . stayed at home less. I've sensed a terrible something growing inside him. I confess to cowardice, Tahath, in ignoring the signs. Thinking, . . . hoping, . . . trusting it to be a passing phase young men experience. I am much at fault. I didn't—couldn't—confront my brother, nor could I even petition Jehovah, lest voicing my fear might somehow make it a horrible reality."

Mala kept her eyes fixed on the roadway at her feet. But she felt the strength of Tahath's gaze as he replied, "A loving heart hesitates to acknowledge the cloud that might shadow its joy. While that hesitation cannot banish the cloud, neither does it *create* the shadow. But what—beyond increasing silence and lessening joy—is there in Abdon that rouses your fear?"

"The answer is an ugly word, Tahath. An ugly spirit. And how unlike the Abdon we both know. But I can put no other identity to it. It is . . . hatred." Mala bit her lip.

After a thoughtful silence Tahath queried, "What or who stands as the object of Abdon's hatred? Has he said?"

"He hates . . . he hates everything! He scorns our house. He resents the necessity for our labors. He rails against our food, our clothing. He upbraids the Romans for their tyranny, but also our own people for their accommodation. This awful thing within him lashes out at all he formerly accepted, at everything he mocked through the years, assuring me that one day it would be different."

Tahath spoke softly. "The kicked dog."

"What did you say?"

"The kicked dog. That's what your description reminds me of. Remember our seeing stray dogs as we grew up, Mala? Boney and pathetic, seeking whatever scraps they could for survival, allowing themselves to be kicked . . . and kicked again. But only so long as they could run away. When cornered, with no way to escape the abuse, they become ferocious: snarling and biting, attacking their attacker, fighting with all the pent-up fury of months and years."

Mala nodded. "That's . . . vivid, Tahath. I hurt to liken my brother to a dog, yet the picture is apt. But why? Why would Abdon suddenly feel himself cornered? Made to fight?"

"That I can't answer. Perhaps there's no single event or cause, but rather an accumulation of life's small cruelties."

"How long will he stand at bay? What good can he accomplish, what change can he force? And when, oh when, Tahath, will he again become my gentle Abdon?"

"No one but Jehovah Himself can answer such questions. None but Jehovah Himself can bring Abdon back into his rightful self. It is to Jehovah we must appeal, Mala. I pledge my help for you in that appeal."

"I'm grateful, Tahath. You're a kind, a good friend." Lengthening her stride and putting a spring into her step, Mala breathed, "Ah, see how the day lightens! And so should my spirit. If one's trust in Jehovah be true, then gloomy thoughts should be passing things, as night's darkness gives way to the day. Tell me now how matters go in your metals workshop." The two continued in comfortable conversation for the duration of their journey.

Soon they entered the city. She felt, as always, rising tension as they moved into already-crowded streets. Most people seemed drawn to the noise, bustle, and excitement of Jerusalem. Not she. She would have been content to stay forever within the quiet of Bethphage. Only financial necessity ever brought her here.

Sensing her unease, Tahath asked, "Would you mind first going to the marketplace with me? I can leave Belshazzar with one of the stall boys, then I'll be free to go with you to your patroness."

Mala's heart lifted. "Of course. I'd be grateful for your company. Thank you."

Now well within the city itself, Mala and Tahath grew quiet; the surrounding noise discouraged further conversation. Jerusalem's every characteristic assaulted Mala's senses. There seemed to be numberless narrow, winding streets. Crowds of people were everywhere: most of them hurried along in swirling currents, some were isolated in knots of conversation, and yet others shouted at one another, hands windmilling. Heavy ox carts vied with Roman chaises borne by ebony slaves, their mistresses lounging within gossamer curtains. Beggars of every sad description called out in querulous voices to heedless passersby. Housewives gossiped loudly from one window to another above the street. With Tahath's reassuring presence, there was a degree of safety from the waves of human activity that threatened to drown her. Glancing at her companion's face, Mala was surprised to see a reflection of her own feelings. Could it be Tahath didn't relish the city either? Abdon so constantly disparaged Bethphage that Mala had come to feel herself alone in preferring village life.

Feeling her gaze, Tahath turned his face briefly toward her, rolling his eyes upward and pulling the corners of his mouth down into a comic expression of dislike. Mala laughed, ridiculously pleased to recognize Tahath's understanding and his shared response. She reached back with one hand to stroke Belshazzar's nose. He plodded stoically along behind them, though his overhanging burden was often bumped and buffeted, sometimes nearly knocking the little donkey off his feet.

So the trio continued to the marketplace. Activity there was at such height one would have thought it noonday rather than early morning. Stalls crowded against one another as far as Mala could see. Each was being dressed for the day in its respective offerings. Merchants piled fruits and vegetables in great baskets. They hoisted newly-slain carcasses of sheep and calves onto meat hooks. They stacked live chickens and ducks in cage upon wooden cage. Several stalls displaying fabrics caught Mala's eye. She was pleased that none seemed to offer as fine a quality or color as that in the garment she carried carefully under her aba.

Tahath gestured toward a stall on the opposite side of the street. They crossed cautiously, rushing the last few steps to avoid oncoming Roman soldiers. Even Belshazzar voluntarily broke into a trot. Once safe, Mala turned to stare, mesmerized, at the mounted figures. She shuddered involuntarily as she pictured similar figures as they must have been on the day of her parents' death, moving into the crowds, horses rearing with flailing hooves, riders yelling, slashing haphazardly with their swords.

"Mala. Mala . . ."

Startled, she dragged her eyes away from the retreating Romans, made herself answer Tahath. "Yes? Oh . . . uh . . . I'm sorry . . ."

"I said we're finished here. We can go now to the Roman section. We'll come back this way later to collect Belshazzar." So saying, he began breaking the way through ever-more-crowded streets. Mala remembered how many times, when alone in Jerusalem, she had become lost trying to find the home of some Roman patroness. There would be no such complications today. Tahath moved confidently and quickly.

The character of the city changed as they neared the Roman section. Voices were self-consciously muted. Jews in the streets moved furtively. Mingled fear and hatred hung in the air like smoke. The buildings, too, were different. Massive edifices proclaimed the Romans' grip upon the land and their intention to keep it. As she did each time she entered the Roman quarter, Mala renewed her heart's prayer for the promised Messiah who would free her people from Roman oppression.

Familiar landmarks brought her mind back to the present. "It's not much farther now, Tahath. Just after the next turning."

When they arrived at the great house, Tahath insisted upon waiting outside for her. A thin servant girl ushered Mala into Lady Terentia's presence, bowing as she announced, "The seamstress with your completed garment, Mistress."

Lady Terentia rose on one elbow among the rich cushions of her couch. Carefully curled and varnished-looking hair framed painted cheeks, aquiline nose, and a pinched mouth whose infrequent smiles never reached the pale, bulging eyes. "Ah. You're early in delivering my order. That pleases me. Now hold it up there where you stand so I can see if the lines of the garment are right." Mala obediently shook the glistening fabric from its folds and held it by the shoulders. She willed herself not to tremble. How she dreaded this awful moment—when a capricious patron might refuse her work . . . and the payment for it. But she relaxed as she noted the smile that came to Lady Terentia's thin lips. "From this distance it appears satisfactory. Step forward now, that I may inspect the workmanship." Mala did so with confidence, knowing her meticulous handwork could seldom be surpassed.

The Roman woman inspected the seams, hem, and finish work. Then she swung her legs off the couch. Holding the chiton against her plump body, she asked, "It suits me, does it not?"

Mala bowed slightly as she replied, "Indeed, Mistress. The color enhances your own."

Obviously pleased, the Roman woman caressed the silk, watching it catch the light. Mala idly wondered what it would be like to live amid the luxury of marble, servants, and silk; to have everything and anything one wanted simply by giving an order. But no envy rose in response to the thought. Her visits to this great house and others like it had made her aware of underlying dissatisfactions and boredom within their splendid walls.

Lady Terentia reclined again. "Here, Challa." She held the garment toward a servant girl. "See this is put away carefully. Perhaps later today I'll have you summon the cobbler. A new belt and sandals of gold would do nicely to complete the costume. And send Hodesh with payment for the seamstress. I shall add a bit to what we contracted for because I am pleased with your work, Jewess, and with your promptness."

Mala inclined her head as she responded, "Thank you, Mistress." With that, she was waved out of the room. She waited near the front door for the servant Hodesh, whose entrance she heard before she saw.

Hodesh, pink-cheeked and harried, puffed her way toward Mala. "Here, girl. Here's your pay." The serving woman moved closer to Mala and lowered her voice. "Little enough by my measure. But Her Ladyship is not generous toward any but herself, I can tell you. By the looks of you, you could do with something extra, and your fine work's certainly worth it! So thinking, I've here a bit of parchment directing you to one who'll not only rightly appreciate but also richly pay for your needle's artistry. The house is nearby, and I've sent one of the scullery girls to let them know of your coming."

"Oh, thank you! I do need more work—"

Hodesh snorted. "It's more *payment* that you need! Hurry along now. You may not be going to your fortune, but you'll certainly come into better than you get here."

"Hodesh! Hodesh, where are you? Come in here at once." Lady Terentia's rasping call carried sharply into the entryway, making a lie of the gracious marble interior.

"Coming, Mistress," Hodesh called. As she turned to go, she shrugged and sighed.

Mala stuffed the coins of her payment into the small leather purse at her waist. Then she hurried into the street, inspecting the parchment scrap Hodesh had given her. Tahath appeared at her side. "That didn't take long. Was Her Ladyship pleased with your work?"

"I don't believe *pleased* is a word that applies to Lady Terentia. Temporarily mollified perhaps, but never pleased. Her payment is scanty, as usual, though slightly more generous than for earlier garments. But see—her chief maid of the household gave me this, telling me to go right away to another Roman lady who is, she says, more agreeable."

"Aha. That sounds promising. Let's move on to make the proof of it."

"You're kind, Tahath. But you need to return to the marketplace. Now that the time with Lady Terentia is past, all ahead must be better. And I managed getting out of the Roman quarter better than coming into it."

"There are more than enough sellers at the stall. They've made it plain that it's my goods they want, not my help. And of course Belshazzar relishes his relaxation, miserable beast that he is."

Mala chuckled, knowing Tahath's disparaging term poorly disguised his affection for the little donkey. "All right then. Again, I'm glad for your company." She glanced once more at the parchment, with Hodesh's hastily-drawn map, then turned left down the street. Tahath's comfortable presence insulated her against the bold stares of Roman men who lounged in doorways or rode over the cobbles on tall horses.

As they waited for a heavy horse-drawn wagon to pass, Tahath said, "May I ask what you plan to do with these latest earnings?"

Mala answered thoughtfully, "I'll try to redeem something from Old Bartholomew. If I can begin replacing our household pieces, Abdon may come to feel more contented."

"I think Abdon's hoped-for contentment is less important at the moment than a new aba for you. Your present cloak must poorly keep out the chill."

Mala frowned. For the second time that day someone was implying that she looked ragged—first Hodesh, and now Tahath. She defiantly lifted her chin. "I don't need your advice about how to spend my wage, Tahath!"

"I meant no insult, little friend. I'm just concerned, that's all. Now lower your nose lest you stumble." Tahath's tone was gentle and teasing.

"Well . . ." Not able to think of an appropriate rejoinder, Mala relaxed from her haughty bearing. The two soon reached the location indicated on the parchment. As Mala hesitated before the door, Tahath patted her on the shoulder with one hand and reached for the great brass knocker with the other. Then he quickly stepped aside so he'd not be seen by anyone answering the door.

As Mala waited, she nervously rolled, unrolled, and rerolled the bit of parchment. Then one of the double doors opened. She looked into the face of an aged manservant. His eyes crinkled more deeply at the corners as he asked, "Yes, miss?"

"I . . . uh . . . I was told at Lady Terentia's house to come here. Hodesh told me. She gave me this." Mala held out the parchment scrap, but the old man waved it aside.

"You're the Jewess who's a seamstress, I take it?" Mala nodded, and he went on, "If you're half the wonder I heard that maid describe, my mistress will be happy to meet you indeed. Come in, child."

CHAPTER 3

Mala passed into the cool marble interior as the servant stood aside for her. He closed the door, then moved ahead to show her the way. The pace of his spindly, gnarled legs gave her time to examine the house through which they moved. The atrium fountain splashed gently amid carefully tended shrubbery. As the servant opened another door, Mala heard a plaintive melody. Advancing into the room, she saw two young dark-skinned servant girls. One played a small stringed instrument; the other, a flute. Mala hesitated, but the old manservant took her gently by the arm and moved with her toward the room's occupants.

"Mistress Diana . . ." At the sound of the servant's voice, the young musicians lowered their instruments and turned curious dark eyes toward Mala. They stepped to either side of a marble chair. "The seamstress spoken of has come." The old man bowed to his mistress as he spoke, then he quietly exited.

The chair's occupant lifted her gaze from a piece of needlework in her hands. As the face came up in its framework of loose golden curls, Mala was startled to find the mistress of the household barely older than her servant girls. Lady Diana's face was the perfection of natural beauty and her sweet expression unlike anything Mala had thought possible in a Roman.

Diana handed her needlework to the servant girl on her left, then reached toward Mala as she said softly, "Welcome. Recommendation of your talents has literally raced into our house. May I ask your name?"

Mala had difficulty finding her voice. In all her months of sewing for Lady Terentia, she'd been called nothing but 'Jewess.' "My name . . . my name is . . . Mala, Your Ladyship."

Diana reached out to clasp both Mala's hands in hers, pulling her close to the chair. "Mala," she repeated. "That's a lovely name, and it suits you. Zikhi, take her cloak and head shawl." She interrupted herself to say to Mala, "Forgive me for my presumption. Do you have time to visit a moment?" Mala nodded dumbly. Her hostess indicated that the servant girl should lay the worn garments aside. She continued, "Yes, your name suits. How lovely you are!" Mala felt hot blood rush to her face. She had never been called lovely, in fact she couldn't remember anyone referring to her appearance at all. "Mikiah, bring a chair for our guest, please."

Mala sank gratefully into the delicately carved chair the servant girl placed for her. Her knees felt weak. She must be dreaming this courtesy! She was in a Roman house; there could be no doubt about that. But here was warmth, and . . . yes, genuine welcome. The gentle voice of her hostess sounded again.

"You look faint, Mala. I fear you must have come far—and on foot?"

Mala tried to rally her scattered senses. "Yes . . . No . . . Not too far. My home is in the village of Bethphage."

Diana smiled, the blue eyes sparkling. "I know the place. My husband has driven me about some of the outlying villages. Bethphage is lovely. How wonderful it must be to live in such a place of quiet."

Heartened by the sincerity in Diana's voice, Mala's confusion ebbed. "I've lived in Bethphage since my birth, and I hope to do so always. My brother mocks its smallness, yearning for the excitement of the city."

Diana shook her head. "Yours is the wiser preference to my way of thinking. My own home village outside Rome is much like yours. Ah, but we must not think sadly."

The two servant girls were instantly beside Diana, compassion evident in their eyes. "Mistress, shall we play again for you? Zikhi has composed a new melody. We've practiced, and—"

Diana gestured the girls away. "There's no need for music right now. Later I'll gladly hear the new song."

Mala's wonder increased as she watched Diana's treatment of the servant girls. This golden young woman defied everything Mala had ever known of Romans.

As Zikhi and Mikiah moved apart to sit on large floor pillows, Diana again focused her attention upon Mala. "You and I can rejoice over similar background settings. I wouldn't have sadness creep into our visit. It's only that the longing for home at times becomes so strong."

Mala nodded. "I feel such a longing each time I come to Jerusalem—which is only a short distance from Bethphage. How much worse it must be for you with weeks of travel between you and your own country. Are you to stay in Jerusalem long?"

"Our tenure is uncertain. My husband Dolphus is a legate, serving as the emperor's agent in Jerusalem. His reports have met with favor, and there are rumors of his duties being expanded. By all accounts, that might mean many more months—even years—here."

The Roman lady's openness moved Mala to similar honesty. "But surely . . . I mean . . . we Jews view the city's occupation as a happy thing for you the conquerors. I never thought . . ."

"That a *conqueror* could be unhappy?" The wry note in Diana's voice was unmistakable. "We Romans do possess, indeed, both wealth and power in our occupation of your people, your land." Diana leaned forward, speaking softly so the servant girls could not overhear. "But Mala, appearances are surface things. Oh, surely, many of our number revel in the tyranny we're encouraged to wield. But underneath it all lies the fact that this is *your* land; these are *your* people. We Romans are aliens. We're obeyed and feared, of course, but all the while we're hated. So it is that conquerors can live richly in possessions but poorly in peace."

Mala could frame no fit response to Diana's confession. She simply held the gaze of her lovely hostess, knowing there was no need to drop her eyes in subservience. Slowly, a smile came to each face; woman's heart had spoken to woman's heart.

Suddenly Mala remembered Tahath. "Lady Diana, forgive me, but there's a friend waiting outside for me."

Diana straightened in her chair. "But of course. I've been thoughtless to keep you so long. Are you, as Terentia's maidservant indicated, willing to construct a few clothing items for us?"

"I'd be happy to do so. If you would see a sample of my work . . ."

Diana shook her head. "I need no sample. The recommendations that preceded you are enough. Added to those are the impressions of your person. I have every confidence in you. I'd like to commission several things, for Mikiah and Zikhi as well as for myself. Are you prepared to take our measurements now?"

The remainder of her time in Diana's house went quickly. Forever afterward the scene remained vivid in Mala's mind: quick measuring

and instructions for the servants' garments, then the jolt of distress
Mala felt when, approaching to take Lady Diana's measurements,
Zikhi and Mikiah stepped ahead of her . . . took, each of them, one of
Diana's arms . . . raised their mistress to a standing position. She was
crippled! This beautiful, sweet aristocrat was crippled! Seeing Mala's
distress, Diana forestalled her embarrassment or apology. "Don't hurt
for me, Mala, though I thank you for your sympathy. These lower
limbs of mine are useless, but they're without pain. Matters could be
far more difficult, could they not?"

Filled with jumbled emotions, Mala completed the various
measurements, took the leather purse Diana held out to her, and
eventually found herself again outside the great front door. Tahath
spoke to her, studying her face with piercing concern.

"Mala, what is it? Was she unkind to you? If she hurt you in some
way—"

"What? Oh, forgive my distraction, Tahath. No. There was
nothing unkind in Lady Diana—or in her entire household. Just the
opposite. I don't . . . I can't . . . understand. Let me tell you."

Mala and Tahath walked slowly back to the marketplace deep in
conversation. Though Tahath made thoughtful responses, Mala still
could not comprehend what she had seen and sensed in the Roman
dwelling. Once in the noisy marketplace, Tahath asked her to wait in
an out-of-the-way corner of the metals shop while he handled some
business matters with the owner. Glad for the chance to sit a moment
and think specifically toward fabrics to be purchased for Lady Diana's
order, Mala decided she needed to learn how much she'd been given
for the purchase. With her mind on possible colors and weights of
cloth, she loosened the drawstrings of the small leather money pouch.
She stared at its contents in disbelief—stared at more money than
she had ever seen at one time in her life. It was not the gold itself that
held her motionless. Rather, it was the trust and confidence the coins
represented. Mala shook her head, trying to clear her mind. Lady

Diana's gold put upon her a great weight of responsibility. Closing the money pouch and fastening it securely at her waist, Mala felt exhilaration, tension, and determination.

As they left the metal seller's stall, it was clear that Tahath knew the entire marketplace well; he exchanged friendly greetings with many of the vendors. He guided Mala to several merchants he considered the best sources for the fabrics she sought. The purchases did not take long. Mala's instincts for quality and beauty were strong. She chose delicate colors in soft but sturdy weave for Zikhi and Mikiah. For Lady Diana she selected a fine woven linen of sky blue. Its subtle sheen would compliment its wearer's eyes, and its considerable body would disguise her withered legs. Completing her transactions with Tahath's help in bargaining, Mala insisted on carrying the parcels herself as they returned to the metals stall. Behind it, Belshazzar stood tethered, head and ears drooping, eyes closed.

Mala laughed at the donkey's exaggerated reactions to Tahath's lashing the bundles of fabric to his empty pack harness. "Belshazzar, you're akin to the mimes who come to Bethphage; you use no words, yet your meaning is clear! One would think to look at you, that these few light bundles were the very weight of the world!"

Tahath joined Mala's laughter. "True. What a wretched fellow!" So saying, he fondled Belshazzar's ear. The donkey leaned his head against his master's caressing hand, his expression now blissful.

The trio was soon on its way, joining the many who were leaving Jerusalem. Mala smiled across Belshazzar's head at Tahath. "To think it is evening! I've never stayed in the city a full day. And yet the time has seemed neither lengthy nor difficult. Thank you for helping to make it so pleasant, Tahath."

Tahath answered with an elaborate shrug. "Accompanying you made my day pleasant as well, Mala. Pleasantness will end abruptly, however, if we don't eat something."

At the mention of food, Mala's midsection rumbled emptily. But she shook her head at Tahath. "I brought no food . . . thinking, of course, that I'd be home before midday." She didn't want Tahath to guess that there had been no food to bring.

Tahath cheerfully began untying a bundle from Belshazzar's load. "I'll not have you collapsing before we reach Bethphage. I have plenty of smoked fish as well as bread. And see—here's the water jug my noble beast has guarded for us all day!"

Mala gratefully accepted Tahath's offer, forcing herself to disguise the intensity of her hunger by eating and drinking slowly as they walked along.

When they came to the edge of Bethphage, Mala spoke. "Now, Tahath, this is far enough for your kind escort. I'll take my parcels."

"Belshazzar and I had planned all along to see you home."

Mala shook her head. "You have spent enough of your time easing my way. You've more than earned your freedom and rest."

Tahath sighed. "I know you too well to argue, Mala. So here are your day's purchases. I wish you well in working for your new patroness."

"Thank you." Mala settled her bundles in one arm, paused, then reached out with a light touch on Tahath's hand where it rested on Belshazzar's head. "I do thank you, Tahath. For today, yes, but for more. King Solomon wrote of a friend's value. Friendship for Abdon and me is rare. Hence, it is treasured indeed. And now, shalom."

Mala quickly moved away into the twilight. Tahath watched her straight, slim back. It fairly shouted independence and determination.

CHAPTER 4

A fortnight had passed since the day in Jerusalem with Tahath. Mala had used most of Lady Terentia's payment to purchase a few essentials for the house. There had not been enough left to redeem anything from Bartholomew, the village moneylender. Nevertheless, her evenings of sewing for the new patroness, Lady Diana, were enhanced by the fact that there was now sufficient charcoal to keep evening's chill at bay.

As she worked, Mala fixed her mind determinedly upon what she was doing and upon those in the Roman household for whom she was constructing the garments. She would not allow herself to think of Abdon, of his failure to come home, of what his continuing absence might mean.

Then all at once one midafternoon he was there again. He burst in upon her with a bellow. "Ho! Sparrow! See? Your brother keeps his word and brings provision for your shabby nest!"

Mala whirled, nearly dropping a newly-baked loaf of bread. "Abdon! At last you've come."

Abdon stood tall, his legs uncharacteristically widespread. "I have come indeed. Hold out your hands." Mala obeyed slowly, dazed by her brother's brittle exuberance. "Here are some crumbs for my Sparrow. See how they glitter?" So saying, he dropped a handful of coins into her cupped hands.

Mala stared, dumbfounded, at the coins. Her voice alternated between a squeak and a whisper. "So much? Where? Where did you? How?"

Abdon's answering laugh was over-loud. "For shame, Sparrow. Don't question the hand that so richly meets your needs. Simply accept. And rejoice."

Mala shook her head. "You've only been but a fortnight. How could you earn so much . . . and your clothing . . . by its appearance?"

Irritation glinted in her brother's eyes. "Questions. Nothing but questions. Are there no thanks, Mala, for what you hold? Is there no kiss for the brother whose love has brought it?"

Mala swallowed over the fearful uncertainty lumping in her throat. "Could you hold . . . these . . . this . . . for a moment?" Handing the coins to Abdon, Mala removed the sash from her waist, held it open for Abdon to pour in the money, then brought its edges together around the coins. Carefully, she laid the bundled riches on a stool. Then she turned and rose to her tiptoes, throwing her arms around her brother's neck. "Forgive me, Abdon. Of course I thank you. It's just that the surprise of your coming . . . of . . . of all this . . . ." She indicated the bundled gold. "You are too good to me, dear brother."

Abdon returned Mala's hug, crushing her to him, burying his face in her hair. "Tell me that my gift pleases you, Sparrow, that it will ease life's hardness."

She drew her head from Abdon's chest, and looked up into his eyes. "Of course. Thank you for wanting to provide for my . . . for our . . . needs here. You're home to stay, aren't you? You'll let me cook for you."

Abdon squeezed Mala, then he held her slightly away, cupped her chin in his hands, and smiled down into her eyes. "The very smell of your fresh bread draws me to stay. It's very nearly irresistible." But then Abdon released his sister, moved away to the room's small window. His voice took on again the strangeness Mala sensed in everything about him. "I would I could remain here. But that's impossible. At least right now. I . . . there are friends who've helped me . . . I must stay there . . . through obligation to them . . ."

"But, Abdon—"

He raised his hand, silencing her protest. "We both must be strong . . . must sacrifice for a time, you and I . . ."

Mala shook her head, mutely appealing to her brother for an explanation.

"We already know the meaning of hardship, Sparrow. This is but another of its faces. This face, though, will be softened—as none has been before—softened by the gleam of gold."

"Oh, Abdon, I would gladly forfeit any gold—and all gold—if we could be together again."

"No!" Mala was shaken by the anger in his shout. He strode to the door. "There is no other way. This thing to be done must be done apart—in order that we might eventually be together. Together and happy and rich! You'll no longer be thin and shabby, like a sparrow. You'll be plump and gorgeous, like a . . . like a peacock!" He went out into the night. The door slammed shut, punctuating his words.

Mala stood unmoving, caught fast in a sense of unreality. Abdon must surely return, must tell her it was a mistake . . . a dream . . . a jest . . . a . . . anything but truth. At last she tore her gaze from the door and moved numbly across the room. She picked up the sash-bound coins. The actual weight was slight, but it burdened her soul. This was wrong—all wrong. Her heart knew certainty, though her mind could not discern a definite shape to the wrong. Abdon's mysterious riches must not be spent. Of that she was sure. Even to touch it was unseemly. But she must hide it. Oh, that neither its glitter nor its frightening, questionable source had ever entered her world!

What place would serve? In her mind she walked through the three small rooms of the house, dismissing one possible hiding site after another. It would have to be here in the main room, bare as it was. Then she knew—only one place would do. And it would do well indeed. She worked slowly and meticulously making the necessary preparations. When all was in order and the gold safely hidden, she went outside and seated herself on the small bench beside the door. She drew in slow, deep breaths of the fresh air. Evening shadows descended, soon to be replaced by full darkness. Feeling neither hunger nor the passage of time, Mala sat in silent misery. At last she re-entered the house, went to bed, and fell into exhausted sleep.

Sleep gave no respite from Mala's mental turmoil, but merely changed its form. Her dreams were peopled with formless, threatening presences that swooped at her, sending her staggering backward toward a yawning abyss. She attempted to ward off the attack, to shield herself, to scream—but still she was pushed back. Mala woke before dawn, trembling and perspiring. She lay unmoving, relieved to find the night's threat unreal, yet burdened with daylight's renewed heartache for Abdon.

Despite her dogged efforts, midmorning found her lagging in her planned sewing schedule. Nothing went well. She repeatedly caught herself sitting with hands idle and eyes fixed, unseeing, on the cloth in her lap. With a sigh she would resume her work. In order to put

thoughts of Abdon out of her mind, she relived her happy time in
Jerusalem with Tahath. His image came readily to mind. Of middle
height, he was stockier in build than Abdon. As playmates in their
younger years, the boys' wrestling matches had usually ended with
Tahath the victor. While he seemed more mature than her brother,
Tahath at the same time evidenced his less than twenty years in his
open, pleasant facial expression and his energetic bearing. Mala was
thankful that childhood's special friendship was continuing so strongly
into this time of troubling youth.

Then her thoughts moved on to Lady Diana. Having met
her, Mala's hatred of Roman occupation had been complicated by
recognition that among the oppressors there were individuals—
likable individuals—who struggled with difficulties on their side
of the situation. How long would foreigners occupy the country,
experiencing self-exile from their own people and lands? How long
must her own people suffer under Roman rule? When would come
the Messiah so long ago promised to them? When were Jehovah's
people to know freedom and prosperity and peace?

Her thoughts were broken by a knock at the door. The rarity of
such a thing in her lonely existence sent a tiny shiver of fear over her.
Mala rose stiffly, carefully laying aside the garments on which she was
working.

The sight of Lady Terentia's maid standing on the stone step
quieted Mala's heart. "Hodesh!" she exclaimed. "Lady Terentia has
never sent you before. Surely you didn't have to walk the distance
from the city."

Hodesh accepted Mala's gestured welcome into the house.
"Better I had walked than to have ridden in that jouncing horse-
drawn contraption out there! My very teeth must be loosened." She
deposited her considerable bulk on the bench Mala indicated. "Ah
well," she added, "perhaps the jostling will have loosened some of my
excess self as well."

"May I give you something to eat or drink?"

"Nothing to eat, but a bit of water would be welcome," said Hodesh.

Mala moved to the scullery corner and poured water from its large clay ewer, then returned and handed the water to the Roman woman.

"Thank you." Hodesh took three swift swallows from the cup and smiled, wiping her mouth with the back of her hand. "Ahh. That makes me feel this morning's trip less grueling."

Mala's brows drew together in a puzzled frown. "But why did your mistress choose to send you? Always before her requests have come by one of the lesser house servants."

Hodesh snorted. "Requests! Lady Terentia doesn't make requests. She only gives orders—gives them to one and all. But that you've observed on your own. This particular charge she wouldn't entrust to any of the other servants. She carried on at great length about the unreliability of all who serve her! That was no compliment to me, I assure you; I simply represent the least in her disfavor at the moment."

Mala could think of no fitting response, so she remained silent.

Draining the last of her water and setting aside the empty cup, Hodesh spoke again. "But now to the business for which I've come. Lady Terentia would be furious could she know how I'm dawdling. Hidden here upon my person is a fabric she commissions you to make up for her before the new moon." So saying, Hodesh carefully drew a length of fabric from under her broad sash.

As she watched the process, Mala at first found it hard to restrain her laughter, for the considerable bulk of hidden material, once removed, barely diminished Hodesh's generous girth. Then as the Roman woman shook out the fabric, the girl's mouth dropped open.

Cloth of gold! She had heard of its existence, but never had she actually beheld any. She was speechless as Hodesh tried to place the material in her hands.

"But I . . . it is too fine . . . too beautiful. And so fragile! I can't do it, Hodesh. My skill is insufficient. I would fear keeping something so valuable here in the house."

Hodesh heaved a great sigh. "Such practical matters don't come into consideration with Lady Terentia. She has *requested* that you make the garment following the same pattern as the green silk you most recently completed for her."

Mala shook her head vehemently. "It's an impossibility. I'd be mad to accept such immense responsibility!"

Hodesh rose and placed a chubby hand on Mala's shoulder. She spoke quietly but firmly. "You would be mad to refuse Lady Terentia. Believe me when I say that it would mean disaster for you. You've heard of Roman cruelty. Don't ask to experience it. Within my mistress there lies a heart immeasurably cold. The slightest provocation can result in this." Hodesh drew up the hem of her tunic, exposing to the knees her sturdily muscled legs. Across them lay great, long welts. The scars' varying hues told their relative age; many had grown white—obviously years old—, others were a paling pink, still others were red in their newness with darkly bruised edges.

Mala's face drained of color; her voice rasped. "She . . . Lady Terentia . . . did that to you?"

Hodesh let her skirt fall again. "Oh, yes. And those were for minor irritations. My back chronicles my worse offenses—as, for instance, when I didn't supervise the cook closely enough, or the seasoning of a pheasant displeased her, or the time—"

"But how could she?"

"This is the point you must understand, child: Lady Terentia not only could and can vent her cruelty at the slightest provocation; more, she delights to do so. Should you refuse her wishes regarding the cloth of gold, she will see to it that you are suitably punished—with suitability dictated by her twisted mind. You dare not deny her."

The two women faced each other silently as Hodesh held out the glistening fabric. Slowly lifting her hands to receive it, the younger woman was swept with a sickening dread. The silence stretched on until Mala at last found her voice. "As awful as the fear and threat this one moment and its commission means for me, your having to endure such things—and unjust punishment as well from your mistress—is . . . is beyond imagining."

"There are better owners, indeed. But as long as my work is fast enough and my demeanor lowly enough, duty to Lady Terentia is survivable. Besides, only weeks remain before I will have earned my freedom."

"And what will you do then? Return to Rome, I suppose, since that is home to you."

Hodesh picked up the empty water cup and turned it slowly in her hands. "Rome? No. My people, of course, think me unbalanced, but I would prefer to remain here."

"In Judea?" Mala could not contain her surprise. "But surely—"

"Lady Terentia's bitter rantings against Judea are constant, and most of our countrymen echo her sentiments. Yet service here has given me years of opportunity to observe Judea and you Jews. This land and its people are unlike Rome and Romans. Of course there is cruelty, suffering, and hatred here as in my homeland. But somehow those things don't predominate. It's as if there's an underlying depth of . . . of quietness or patience or . . ." Hodesh ended by shrugging her shoulders.

Mala nodded. "I'm grateful you feel that quietness to be a positive thing. We're often derided as spiritless and cowardly. Those charges are made not only by Romans, but also by some of our own people who would have us rise up in rebellion. My parents, though, looked differently upon our subjugation and your Roman rule. They pointed out again and again that our two peoples' contrast both in national essence and in social power has a single source—our differing *worship*."

"Worship? How so?"

"My father said that the spiritual focus of a people ultimately determines everything about that people. He pointed out examples at every opportunity. You Romans are ever striving, reaching out in all directions to gain, to conquer, to achieve. Roman religion gives rise to all those by the character of its many gods and by what those gods demand of their followers."

Hodesh nodded. "It's true that most of our gods are themselves striving and angry. So of course it's necessary to please and placate them."

"But isn't it wearisome to be always struggling—whether in political conquest or in personal worship?"

Hodesh's answer came slowly, thoughtfully. "Wearying. Though I never thought of it that way, you may have a point. So then the greater . . . quietness . . . of your people, which has become a thing to keep me here in Judea, has its source in your religion?"

"Yes. We *rest* in the belief that there is but one God, Jehovah. He is a God of love, and He calls us in love simply to obey Him. That point marks cause for our differing social positions with you Romans as rulers and we Jews as your subjects. My people have failed to obey Jehovah, and we are suffering the hard consequences our prophets foretold."

Hodesh's face was thoughtful as she listened to Mala. Then she shook herself as though to loosen concentration's hold. "But I must return to Jerusalem quickly, or my punishment will bear out the warning I've given you." Hodesh placed her cup on the bench and hurried toward the door. Opening it, she spoke again to Mala. "Remember—the garment must be delivered before the new moon." With that she was gone.

Mala stood unmoving until the sounds of departing wheels, harness, hooves, and metal faded. She stared at the gossamer, gleaming mass she held in her hands. It seemed to her a golden web in which she was caught and held, helpless against a great crouching spider. Her heart began to race as she realized the immediate danger: someone seeing or hearing of the priceless fabric, coming to steal it from her. Again she was forced to hide something she did not even want to have. Again she mentally assessed her limited options. Her decision was to guard the cloth with her very life. She wrapped it in a large piece of her own homespun and placed it carefully under her thin straw sleeping mat.

At last she returned to her work on the garments for Lady Diana's household, her jaw set. Regardless of the golden cloth and the demanded time for its completion, Mala was determined that the crippled Roman lady's commission would be finished first. But the fear that had entered the house with the precious fabric lent a swiftness to her fingers which had been missing before Hodesh's arrival. As her needle flew, so did her mind in constructing both a schedule and a setting to prevent anyone's glimpsing the cloth of gold. Her normal routine would have to be altered. No more sewing close to the window in daylight hours; no leaving the garment lying on her stool while she went about some chore to relieve cramping muscles. Though visitors were rare, she would have to guard against discovery in that eventuality as well. Scraps . . . that was it! She would construct a large bag from the scraps of the several garments now in progress, keep it constantly by her while she worked on the priceless gold, and slip the rich stuff quickly out of sight in the bag if there should be a knock at the door.

Suddenly the imagined knock became real. Her heart gave a frightened lurch. The knock sounded again. She set aside her work, straightening her sash and trying to compose her face as she moved to answer the door in this, a most unusual, second visit to her small house.

Relief filled her at sight of Tahath. "Oh, Tahath!" she exclaimed. "I'm so glad it's you."

"I judge that whoever else you thought here at your door would have been rather unpleasant. Has someone been bothering you? Just tell me who it is, and I'll—"

"No, no. No one is bothering me. I just had a rather unpleasant commission brought to me, and I thought perhaps there might be . . . But now I'm unmannerly. Won't you have a seat there on the bench? I can't, of course, invite you into the house." Blushing slightly at the awkward moment, Mala rushed on, "But I'll join you in just a moment with some refreshment, and we can talk."

"I would like that," Tahath said as he moved to the tree-shaded bench.

Mala placed a cluster of grapes, a small wedge of goat cheese, and two cups of water on her only tray. She carried it carefully out the door and to the bench where Tahath waited. She sat down, placing the laden tray between them. Tahath explained that he had come to offer to deliver any of her completed sewing projects on his intended trip into Jerusalem the next day. Mala thanked him, regretting that several more days of work were required before any garments could be completed. Then as they ate, Mala recounted the tale of Hodesh's visit. Tahath's face grew increasingly somber as he listened.

"It worries me that you accepted the commission, Mala."

"But as I told you, Hodesh made it clear that there's no choice. If you could have seen her scars!" Mala shivered at the memory.

"Such cruelty is unthinkable in a woman—even a Roman woman!" Tahath flung an empty grape stem against the tree.

"I've always sensed hardness in Lady Terentia, but to learn of its awful nature and extent . . . And if she treats Hodesh so—Hodesh who is faithful in herself and in her work—what must the lesser servants endure?"

"Cruel treatment for those of her own household is one thing, but for her to threaten you—"

Mala interrupted. "The threat wasn't direct, Tahath. In fact it was only Hodesh's kindness that warned of danger by displeasing Lady Terentia."

Tahath rose so abruptly from the bench that the food tray with its water cups tipped crazily. Mala reached out a steadying hand. After a moment of agitated pacing, Tahath came to a halt facing her. His voice was stern when he spoke. "Whether direct or indirect, the threat is real. You and I have lived long enough and seen enough to know how readily the Romans bring harsh measures against us who are their conquered people." He turned away suddenly and began to pace again. "And aside from threatened punishment, there's also the present danger of discovery." Tahath returned to sit on the bench. He lowered his voice as he continued, "Discovery of the priceless fabric forced upon you."

Mala sighed. "Having that in my house is the thing that most concerns me. But I'll take great care not to let anyone see it or even guess that it's here."

Tahath frowned. "Still, Bethphage is a small village, and things considered secret too often become known almost while they happen. It's as if the air itself wafts tales from one house to another!"

"It's more accurate to suspect *water* instead of air, Tahath; water that goes to every house in the village, carried by the women who gossip at the well." Mala smiled as she spoke.

But Tahath refused to be distracted by her attempt at lightness. "Whatever the means, there are few if any secrets in Bethphage. So you must be protected."

"Protected!" Mala blurted the word, puzzlement on her face.

Tahath held up his hand to forestall her further comment. "Yes, protected. While that treasure of fabric is in your house, you, the house, and the fabric must have a special guard mounted against any possible thievery."

"But what?"

"Leave that to me. I have good and true friends. You'll have no need to fear for safety—either for yourself or for the golden cloth." Suddenly Tahath grinned. "Now that we have things settled, I believe I'll finish that cheese. Then I must be on my way."

As he resumed eating, Mala's heart constricted with gratitude for such stalwart friendship. "You're too kind by far, Tahath. I tried not to be afraid, but Hodesh's scarred legs . . . and the value of such fabled fabric . . . I've been quaking inside. How can I thank you for making the world come right again?"

Tahath cleared his throat. "It's what any friend would do, Mala— no more. And as for thanking me—that you can do by working *quickly* on that cloth of gold and returning it to Jerusalem!"

Chapter 5

Days melted into one another. Mala's work on the garments for Lady Diana's household, plus her nerve-straining efforts on Lady Terentia's cloth of gold, demanded both concentration and speed. But the work had its benefits too, for filled hours did not drag nor did they allow leisure for tortuous thoughts of Abdon.

As she worked late into each night, bending close to the oil light, Mala felt secure in Tahath's pledged protection. Occasionally she would hear small, reassuring sounds in the outside darkness: a quiet tread of passing and repassing feet, a shuffle of changing body positions, or a stifled yawn. Surely Jehovah had smiled upon her when she and Abdon had become friends with Tahath.

Mala had often wondered about Tahath's parents. Nothing had ever been said of his family, except that he had none. Nor was Tahath native to Bethphage. He had come to the village only shortly before she and Abdon met him. It was unusual in Jewish society for a child to be abandoned as Tahath apparently had been, particularly since both his character and his training in metalwork were clearly superior. But Bethphage was marked by a spirit of easy acceptance toward those rare individuals who chose to settle there. Whatever his roots, Tahath had been assimilated into village life without personality conflicts or negative gossip.

From the time of her parents' death Mala lived in constant awareness of being different. The three friends were misfits in Bethphage's warm family atmosphere. Though residents of the village were kind, there was always that moment in the evening when the men came in from field or market, going home to their families. From one end of the village to the other, waning daylight was filled with conversation and laughter, adult voices mingled with children's . . .

Mala abruptly called a halt to her useless musings. She could not allow her mind to continue along this thought path lest she be overcome by brooding questions about Jehovah's dealings. Instead, she must hold firmly to what her mother and father had taught while they were alive—that Jehovah was infinitely good, limitless in His wisdom, and always perfectly balancing mercy and truth as He worked circumstances together for His Name's sake. And yet . . . How could the past years of aching loneliness come to good? And now to that burden had been added the misery of Abdon's abandonment.

Mala shook her head and squared her shoulders. Abandoned though she be for the time, it only meant she must prove herself capable of independence. She would not crumple, and she certainly would not rely upon the gold Abdon had so strangely supplied. Rather, she must seek more customers for her sewing. She would ask Lady Diana for references among her Roman friends. She could also use her scraps of both time and leftover fabrics in order to construct small, useful things like sashes—items she could barter here in the village.

All at once the night's quiet broke into shards of sound. Through the window came a confusion of voices, grunts, gasps, soft thuds, and a woman's stifled shriek. Mala bolted up from her stool, dropping everything from her lap. Panicky, she stooped to stuff the golden garment into its concealing scrap bag. The door burst open, and a strange assortment of bodies came through it in a flood.

"May a man not visit his own sister's house without being set upon?" Abdon shouted the question, and red-faced, he attempted to straighten his clothing from its obvious disarray.

"Forgive me, Abdon, but I was too sleepy to recognize you out there in the dark." Tahath too was straightening his tunic and sash. "And the approach of so many startled me."

As Tahath and Abdon moved into the room, the rest of the group came into view. Mala gaped, amazed. They were wholly unlike anyone who had ever entered the house before that moment.

There were two men and between them a woman whom Mala guessed to be about her own age. As the trio advanced toward the center of the room, Mala instinctively took a quick step backward. Then, embarrassed, she bent to collect her various sewing items where they had dropped. But the awkwardness of her automatic retreat had apparently gone unnoticed; the three newcomers were intent upon the exchange between Abdon and Tahath.

"Who is this lout who dares attack you upon your own doorstep, Abdon? And why don't you punish his insolence? We'd be happy to assist you in that! Village clod!" The speaker was a burly, dark-skinned man whose abundant hair showed slightly silver at the temples. His eyes were like glittering black onyx as he scowled at Tahath.

"No punishment is needed. This fellow is friend to me and to my sister. Apparently he was doing guard duty, though I'm not sure why."

Mala at last found her voice. "I can explain, Abdon. Tahath has been kind enough . . ." Words and voice evaporated as the man who had spoken earlier strode across the room toward her. Mala clutched the items she had rescued from the floor, willing herself not to tremble. The stranger came close—too close; his physical bigness made Mala feel dwarfed. Worse, his breath smelled of strong wine.

He stared at Mala in silence, then his lips lifted in a slow, one-sided smile. "Do explain, little sister, for surely you are that one of whom Abdon has spoken. Your voice falls fair on my ear. Abdon, why didn't you tell me your sister was a beauty? This shall be a pleasant visit indeed."

The man's dark stare held Mala's eyes, but she slowly moved away, crossing to stand beside Abdon. He put his arm protectively about her shoulders. "Mala is my little sparrow—not to be sought by an eagle like you, my friend."

Ignoring Abdon's verbal jab, the big stranger again crossed to Mala where she stood enfolded by her brother's arm. "Come, Abdon. We're friends—business partners—are we not? Since I share with you—as for instance I have done with Keturah, here (he swung a careless gesture toward the girl who had entered with them)—so you must share with me; particularly by allowing me to . . . uh . . . enjoy your family."

Tahath shook off the amazement that had made him a silent spectator. He quickly moved close to Mala's other side, inserting himself as a barrier between her and the stranger. "Abdon, as things got out of hand outside, so they threaten to do now inside as well."

The dark stranger shifted his focus from Mala to Tahath and seemed about to attack him either physically or verbally. Then with visible effort, he took a step backward and gave an exaggerated shrug. "Ah well, at the very least, Abdon, you could present us to your sister."

Still with his arm tightly about Mala, Abdon proceeded with introductions. "Mala, Tahath. These are my friends from the city. My . . . the lady . . . is Keturah. Beside her is Dalan. And this is . . . Ben-Oni."

Mala fought to steady her voice as she responded with the hospitality demanded. "You . . . are welcome. Friends of Abdon's are of course friends of mine."

Ben-Oni caught Mala's hand and pulled her from Abdon's embrace. Tahath moved to stop the action, but Abdon put a restraining hand on his arm. Reluctantly, Tahath stayed where he was, watching Ben-Oni through narrowed eyes as the big man moved and spoke.

"Mala, we revel in your welcome, don't we, friends? But come, let me make a more complete introduction." He led Mala to where the other two stood near the still-open door. "This," he indicated the man, "is Dalan the Adroit. All of Jerusalem opens to him and extends the hand of generosity." In response to the introduction, Dalan bowed slightly. In contrast to Ben-Oni's dark bigness, he was fair of skin and slight in build. Seeing him at close range, Mala sensed tremendous energy and barely controlled tension. Although she could not determine the exact color of Dalan's eyes, she reacted against their pale, indirect gaze.

Ben-Oni pulled her forward another step, until she stood face-to-face with Keturah. Mala drew in her breath at the hardness and hostility evident in the young woman. "And here is the flower in our midst. Isn't that true, Keturah? Your spirit has all the softness of newly-opened petals, eh?"

Keturah's dark eyes, rimmed heavily with kohl, blazed at Ben-Oni. "What would the likes of you know of flowers and petals? Strange how prettily you can talk when the mood takes you." With a toss of her head, Keturah broke away and crossed to Abdon. Ben-Oni frowned but did not call her back.

"At any rate, that's the extent of our group that has invaded your house. Since Abdon seemed slow to make proper introductions, I have taken it upon myself. Have I done satisfactorily?" He addressed the entire room.

Nervously, Mala turned from Ben-Oni. "I regret that there's little food here to offer you. My work on several sewing commissions has been so constant that I've had no time . . ."

Again Ben-Oni took control. "Abdon told us of that likelihood, so we have come prepared. Keturah—the basket!"

Keturah sulkily went to the doorway and retrieved a large basket Mala had not noticed. Holding the basket, Keturah glanced scornfully around the small, bare room, then moved to the table and began unpacking the contents. There were many fruits, as well as several different cheeses. Mala's mouth watered; she saw such things in the markets and knew their cost to be dear. Yet while the foods attracted her physically, they repelled her heart. Like Abdon's gold, which lay hidden so close, these provisions, too, raised a question as to their source. So much seemed wrong here! She looked at Abdon. He had assumed the new, practiced stance that Mala was coming to detest—thrown-back shoulders, raised chin, and weight self-consciously upheld by widespread legs. His eyes, too, heightened Mala's uncertainties. They lacked the old, familiar crinkling at the edges that bespoke humorous interpretation of his surroundings; instead, the lids were partially lowered as if he were measuring everything in view—and found it wanting.

Mala felt herself suddenly adrift—cut loose from moorings of all that was familiar and comfortable. There was no freedom to return to Abdon's side—this strange Abdon. Dalan and Ben-Oni filled her with a dread she'd never known before. And the girl Keturah had obviously laid claim to Abdon and resented everything about Mala's counterclaim. Then Mala looked at Tahath, and a tiny spark of encouragement was kindled in her otherwise darkened heart. There he stood, warmly familiar in every detail of appearance and spirit. At that very moment, Tahath's eyes caught her gaze; he raised his eyebrows in a quizzical expression and blinked rapidly. The unspoken message was clear—his being at a loss with what was going on around them and his sharing her response toward it. Some of Mala's tension ebbed.

Her restored calm was brief, broken once again by Ben-Oni's overpowering presence. He caught her hand and attempted to pull her to the food-laden table. "Come now, let our rightful hostess act her part."

But Mala resisted. "You're welcome to eat yourselves, of course, and I urge you to do so. But I'm not . . . I wish nothing myself right now."

Ben-Oni's eyes sparked angrily, and a dark flush rose in his face. His next words were spoken slowly, as if each one were held on a tight rein. "If the hostess will not partake, neither shall we—this time. The hour is, after all, late."

Keturah made a protesting noise. "What? All this food carried so far . . ."

"I'm sorry. Let me help you return it to the basket. Or, please, I should be happy to have you eat it here." Mala felt constrained to offset the awkwardness she'd created.

Ben-Oni's voice was lower than it had been before, and its intensity was unmistakable. "There will be no eating here tonight, Keturah—as I already said." But as she moved to remove the food from the table, he stopped her, again with the cold power of his speech. "Nor will we take the food away with us. I've offered it to Mala, and it shall remain here until she deigns to eat it. Perhaps after she enjoys this first contribution to her well-being, she'll be more . . . hospitable."

Abdon at last exerted himself. "While I regret my sister's lack of hospitality, we didn't come here with eating uppermost in our minds. Keturah, give her the fabric. Tell her how you wish to have it constructed, then we'll be on our way."

Keturah reached again into the basket and brought out a small bundle. She shook out a length of fabric and held its deep scarlet sheen against her body. "Abdon bought this for me, and he insists that you can make it with finer detailing and more durable construction than anyone else. He won't hear otherwise. So, to please him . . ."

"But I . . ." Not only did Mala's heart revolt in the general sense, but she felt repugnance toward the fabric itself. It seemed the color of blood. She looked pleadingly to Abdon. "I have several commissions here already and, as you can see, I'm busy day and night."

When Abdon spoke again, his voice echoed the hardness of Ben-Oni's. "Though we've overlooked your ill manners as hostess, Mala, we'll not accept your reluctance as seamstress. I've chosen this fabric, Keturah desires it made into a garment, and you will do the sewing."

Tahath took a step forward and began, "But, Abdon—"

His protest was cut off by an angry gesture from Abdon. "It shall be as I've said."

Tears rose to Mala's eyes and a choking lump to her throat. Her heart ached at her brother's coldness. Unable to speak, she went to Keturah, took the fabric from her hands, refolded it and placed it with the other sewing projects.

Ben-Oni broke the heavy silence. "Then our business—for this night—is finished. But now that we've been introduced to your sister, Abdon, we must plan future visits. I'll look forward to better acquaintance, Mala."

Still unable to summon her voice in answer, Mala nodded. Then she stood wrapped in numbing misery as the group disappeared into the night. The manner of their going was in itself a source of pain, for as Ben-Oni and Dalan exited together in murmured conversation, Keturah caught Abdon's hand, wrapped his arm around her waist, and pulled him toward the door as she cast a triumphant backward glance at Mala.

Tahath followed close upon the heels of the group. But as he closed the door he paused briefly to say, "Tomorrow, if I may, I would ask you to come to my shop. There we can discuss tonight's happenings. Will you come, Mala?"

The contrast between the harshness that had gone before and Tahath's warm concern was palpable. Nevertheless she could only nod agreement. Long minutes after quiet had returned to the little house, she gave vent to tears of hurt and confusion.

Since her churning emotions made further work impossible, Mala made ready for bed. The aching weariness she felt went far deeper than the physical; it engulfed both mind and heart. But despite her exhaustion she lay awake for hours. When at last sleep came, it held her only in brief, intermittent snatches, from each of which she wakened trembling. Despite her weariness, she greeted dawn's arrival with relief.

Mala yearned to go to Tahath as soon as his shop would be open for the day's work. But she restrained herself and instead alternated diligent sewing efforts between the two Roman commissions. Reluctantly, too, she fashioned Keturah's scarlet fabric. She felt as if it retained something of the woman who would wear it—a subtle, conniving strength; a hard, expensive quality that transformed intended beauty into ugliness. How could Abdon have come into possession of enough money to purchase such silk? How, indeed, could he afford to maintain friendship with a woman like Keturah? Instinct told Mala that the woman's clinging, proprietary spirit toward Abdon was not only manipulative but also bespoke a fragile relationship made up of selfish demands which, if not satisfied, could be instantly dissolved.

Shortly after midday Mala gathered up Ben-Oni's exotic foods, returning everything to the basket from which they had been taken. She had no appetite, and she was determined not to keep the unfamiliar, rare foods in her house. Their presence kept the memory of last night painfully alive.

Mala did not go directly to Tahath's workplace. Instead she walked to the far edge of Bethphage—the end of the village that lay farthest from Jerusalem. As she had done a number of times through the years, she left the basket and its contents for the Nameless One. He was Bethphage's only beggar—a dark, large but physically twisted man whose eyes, looking out through a matted forelock, were devoid of human sense. Mala went within a few feet of his doorway and set down her offering. He darted from inside, convulsively seized upon the basket, and dragged it into his low hovel.

Mala felt no fear of the man. Though obviously demented and occasionally beset with fits of wild ranting, he was generally gentle and shy. The Nameless One had been a part of Bethphage as long as she could remember. Her parents had taught Abdon and Mala to pity him. They pointed out that his condition should remind them of Jehovah's kindness in granting full mental capacity to the great majority of His human creatures. There was also a responsibility to be kind to those who, like him, were less fortunate. He had never harmed any but himself; his disheveled appearance and wordless rantings constituted a world bounded by the most basic needs of existence. He lived from day to day on alms from compassionate villagers and passersby. Money was meaningless to him . . . but food, clothing, a bit of wood or discarded metal—those were his treasures.

Mala thought of the Nameless One as she moved on toward the little line of Bethphage's workshops. She was shocked to realize that she fleetingly considered him with envy. How simple—and painless—life must be if one's mind were incapable of worry, of striving, of loving!

Her bleakness ended when someone called her name. "Mala! Come close and see the fabrics I've been fortunate enough to acquire. See this piece—as fine as you can find in Jerusalem, I wager! If you'd apply your talents and make it into a garment of average size, I could display it here and share its purchase price with you."

"Thank you for your offer, Zillah." Although she was impatient to move on to Tahath's shop, she did the cloth merchant the courtesy of stepping close to inspect the fabric she was holding. "It's fine indeed. And the color would be pleasing on women of various complexions."

Zillah beamed. She was a large, kind woman whose widowhood had some years ago forced her to make a public business of what she had earlier undertaken in private. Because of her long residence in Bethphage and her good reputation as a housewife, she had been easily accepted among the merchants here in the village's tiny market section. Mala had worked with Zillah in informal partnership occasionally in the past. Several times it had rescued Mala from serious need.

"So you'll make such a garment? There are several newcomers to Bethphage seeking the services of a seamstress. Who better to reap the harvest of their need than you and I in league?"

Mala shook her head, returning the fabric to Zillah's hands. "Thank you for your confidence and for your kindness, Zillah. But lately I find myself with so many commissions I can hardly manage them."

Zillah eyed the girl speculatively. "Then you've already been found by those newcomers of whom I spoke?"

"No, my friend. Abdon first brought me word some months ago of a Roman woman in Jerusalem seeking a seamstress. After completing several assignments satisfactorily, I've recently been put in contact with another Roman household."

"Ah—commissions from Jerusalem! I had wondered at the infrequency of your visits to my shop. Now I understand."

"I do appreciate being kept busy, Zillah. But I would much prefer my commissions to come from and to keep me here in Bethphage! Neither Jerusalem nor its inhabitants hold great attraction for me."

Zillah clucked sympathetically. "Romans hold little attraction for any of us—whether in the city or out of it. You would be wiser to my mind, if you were to discontinue working for the foreigners and concentrate on opportunities for employment right here in the village."

"That's what I yearn to do. Bethphage is world enough for me. But necessity's cords have become bindings of commitment. Until I can somehow loose myself, I must continue as I am. To do otherwise would be dishonorable."

"You're right in that, of course. But know there's expanding opportunity right here to sustain both of us. You're the finest seamstress in Bethphage, and though I'll have to use a lesser skill temporarily, I'll reserve partnership for you alone."

Mala could not keep sadness from her voice as she replied, "I can't thank you sufficiently for that kindness, Zillah. It warms my heart, and it gives me hope for the future—hope recently grown faint."

Zillah angrily slapped a hand on the top of the newly-refolded fabric she had shown to Mala. "I don't wonder you've battled with discouragement! Word of Abdon's leaving is passing back and forth here in the marketplace. Not one of us can understand it! He has always been so faithful."

Mala was stung to defend her brother. "He's faithful still, Zillah. It's the *manner* chosen for his faithfulness that so concerns me. Please tell those who talk of Abdon that he has not abandoned me. I don't want his name dishonored. Surely soon Abdon will explain his mind in the matter, or he'll come back to the old, happier way, or . . ."

"Hmph. For both your sakes I hope that may prove true. But I've walked life's path considerably longer than you, Mala, and what I've seen along that pathway does little to make me share your hope. But there, forgive me. I wouldn't put upon you a greater burden of mind than you already carry. I'm your friend; let it stand at that."

Mala patted Zillah's sturdy arm. "Nor could a thing stand taller in my heart than your friendship. If the time comes soon when I can join our efforts, I'll be happy indeed. But for now I must hurry on. Shalom."

"Shalom, my little friend." With that, Zillah turned and set about straightening her wares.

Mala hurried on down the street. She had to pass only a few more shops before she arrived at the metalworker's. She had barely reached the door before Tahath put aside the plowshare on which he had been working. He came toward her, removing his leather apron as he did so. As he hung the apron on its peg, he spoke to the other two men working in the shop. "I'll be gone briefly. Finish those smaller pieces, then pack them for my trip to Jerusalem two days hence. If I'm needed, you can find me at the enclosure fronting on the synagogue." Then he joined Mala and they moved on along the street side by side.

"You go to Jerusalem again so soon?"

"Jehovah has blessed me with diligent workers here in the shop and with interested buyers in the city's greater marketplace. So Belshazzar and I must endure the crowds."

"I've nearly completed the cloth of gold for Lady Terentia, and I've one garment each for Lady Diana and her servant girls. Would it be possible for me to accompany you so that I can deliver the clothing items? I don't want to hamper your day's business, but you were so helpful last time."

Tahath grinned. "Of course you may go! I'm delighted that you ask. I'll warn Belshazzar to practice his good behavior. Ah, here we are."

They had reached the low wall encircling the synagogue property. Tahath led to a spot where a great tree threw its shade onto the wall. They took a seat side by side on top of the wall, comfortable in the ease of long friendship.

"I'm sorry you had to witness that scene with Abdon and his group last night," Mala began, but Tahath interrupted.

"I've no regret. In fact, I'm glad to have been there—to see for myself the strange person Abdon has become and his even stranger friends. It's no wonder your relationship with your brother has been damaged."

Mala looked at Tahath intently. "Then my reactions aren't exaggerated?"

"Rather I'd say they're quite accurate. In fact my own concern is much greater after what I saw last night."

"But what's to be done? Even when he comes alone, Abdon seems deaf to anything I say."

Tahath thought for a moment before replying. "*Deaf* is an accurate term. It seems Abdon has chosen deafness—not only to your appeals, but also to everything and everyone having to do with his yesterdays. It's as if he has deliberately moved into another room of existence— one barricaded against the past."

"But surely there's some way to breach the barricade. The room he has chosen frightens me. While we're shut out of it, I fear those inside really care nothing for him."

As Tahath nodded his agreement, Mala shivered. "There's such . . . such coldness in those people! How can Abdon, so warm through the years, be drawn to them?"

"I've chased that question around and around in my mind since last night. But like you, I find no answer."

"Then there's no way we can help Abdon?" As Mala framed the query, tears overflowed her eyes and slid down her cheeks.

"We mustn't abandon hope, Mala." Tahath's voice had the ragged edges of tightly-reined emotion. "And we should—indeed we must—turn the matter over to Jehovah."

"But I *have* been praying. Constantly!" Mala protested.

"As have I, but our prayers must change. Rather than petitioning Jehovah with one hand while grasping for human solutions with the other, we each must raise *both* our hands in petition."

"You make me remember words spoken by my mother long ago. I don't remember why, but I was terribly earnest about something, and gesturing wildly; Mother caught my hands in hers and held them. She said, 'Mala, some things lie within our reach as human beings; others lie only within God's.' "

"Exactly. Abdon's *heart* has chosen a new room of life. We can stand crying and begging at the barricaded door to no avail. But Jehovah can reach into that room at any moment, unhampered by the barricade, because He does so from *above*."

Silence fell between Mala and Tahath, but it was the quietness of understanding. Mala's tears had dried. She knew Tahath had hit upon the truth; she determined to resume prayer efforts for her brother in the spirit of utter dependence upon Jehovah.

Tahath cleared his throat. "I asked you to meet me today not *only* that we might talk of Abdon, Mala. There is another matter."

Mala's eyes, which had been fixed unseeing into the distance came back to focus on Tahath's face. She was surprised to see that his forehead was beaded with perspiration though the day was cool. Puzzled, she addressed his uncompleted sentence. "Another matter?"

"Yes. It has to do with . . . it concerns . . . uh . . . your parents . . ."

At the unexpected mention of her father and mother, Mala focused her eyes upon a tiny plant growing in a crevice between stones of the wall on which she sat. She pulled the bit of greenery from its place and slowly began to tear it apart. "What about my parents?" She asked the question without looking up.

"Yours is a fine heritage, Mala." She nodded as Tahath paused and seemed to search for words. He cleared his throat. "While nearly everyone in Bethphage was kind to me when . . . when I came here, your mother and father were especially so."

"Aye. It was, I think, that Abdon and I claimed you as our own from that very first moment we saw you. You so suddenly appeared at the edge of the field. We were tired of waiting for Father to end his day of reaping, and your coming not only brought something new for our interest, but much to rouse our curiosity as well."

Tahath grinned. "Both of you made that quite plain. How your questions flew at me! I could hardly draw breath."

"I thought afterwards that it was well Father was working at the far side of the field. Else he would have reminded us all too plainly that we were being unmannerly toward you."

"Yet your questions were used to good purpose. By the time your father finished his work and joined us, he was able to gather my entire history from your lips. I treasure the memory of his kind heart as he immediately offered that evening's meal at your house, and how, between them, your parents arranged for my lodging and work with Zichri."

"Our family talked much afterwards of Jehovah's provision for you. There you were—come to the village just as Zichri needed an apprentice in his metals shop."

"Certainly it was Jehovah's rich provision," Tahath agreed. "Bethphage offered stability for me at last . . ."

Mala recognized and identified with the note of wistfulness in his voice. The life he'd known prior to his arrival in their village had immediately earned their sympathy. It had also created a special strength in friendship's bond after her own parents' death. Tahath had been orphaned by a storm at sea. He and his family had sailed from Sidon, intending to worship and perhaps even take up residence in Jerusalem. But as the ship neared Joppa, a sudden, raging storm had driven their vessel landward, where it was dashed to pieces against the cliffs. Tahath's mother, father, and sister had perished. After his rescuers had delivered him to Joppa, Tahath had courageously made his way toward Jerusalem, compelled to complete the journey begun with his family.

As if able to discern her thoughts, Tahath continued his reminiscence. "Had Bethphage not opened its doors to me, I'd have gone on into Jerusalem itself and been swallowed up in city life. How thankful I am to have avoided that. The village here gives access to the city but at the same time protects us from its noise and busyness." He changed positions abruptly as if willing himself forward in thought. "So then, the past here has been good to me. And as I've said, much of that goodness sprang from your parents' acceptance of me. Now . . .

er . . . I've never known of any others in your family . . . uh . . . say a
brother of your mother or father . . ."

"I've hardly known of such myself. Both Father and Mother came
from families narrowed by failure to produce sons."

"So there's no one who . . . to whom . . . no kinsman to act
in your behalf in . . . in case of some . . . some formal . . . or legal
matter?"

"There's one who might do so, if it were necessary, but . . ."

"And who is that?"

Mala tore the last tiny branch from the plant in her hands. "The
husband of my father's sister. However, he has shown himself to be
less than eager to assist us in any way."

"How do you mean?"

"When Abdon and I were left orphans, our Uncle Thadeus came
to Bethphage once only, and he made it clear that he'd not consider
taking us in or offering help of any significance."

"What manner of man would respond so coldly?"

"One whose every look, word, and act shows him to be without
warmth."

"But surely for the sake of his wife, your father's sister . . ."

"He's her second husband. She was widowed while young, and
Father said that in marrying her, Thadeus sought less to relieve her
loss than to relieve the thinness of his own purse."

"Still, mightn't he be willing just to represent you in a matter of
custom?"

"Custom? But what . . ."

"Mala, were you and I not orphans, I'd not speak to you as I am at this moment. If indeed your Uncle Thadeus and Zichri, as my guardian of sorts, would each agree to deal in behalf of you and me, would you be willing . . . would you consider? . . ."

"Tahath, what are you trying to say?"

"We're friends, are we not? Good friends and of long standing?"

"Of course we're friends. In fact, Tahath, I don't know how I could survive these days were it not for your friendship."

"I wish to go on being your friend. A better friend. More than a friend. May we move forward toward betrothal?"

As Tahath's halting sentences tumbled over each other and their meaning struck home to Mala, she felt a jolt of utter surprise. Having just come to a settledness about Abdon, here she was moments later sent into emotional disarray. She could only stare at Tahath, her mouth open. "Betrothal?" she finally whispered.

Tahath nodded, his eyes holding hers with a look that suddenly made Mala's heart do strange things.

"But, Tahath, I . . . we . . . There is no dowry."

"Had I wanted dowry, Mala, I could have sought the hand of one of those others in town whose fathers are eager to pass them along to the care of a husband. It's not dowry I want, but you. You who—"

Mala held up both hands in protest. "No, Tahath, please. No more. As you've asked—in friendship—that we become betrothed, so I must reply—in friendship—that I cannot."

"But why?"

"Because it would be cruel and unfair."

Tahath tried to protest, but Mala stopped him with a gesture. "No, let me go on. A wife with no dowry I must necessarily be, if ever I become a wife. But there must not be the added hardship of a wife who has neither heart to give in love nor hands to give in care because heart and hands are reaching toward her brother."

"I want to help carry your burden for Abdon, Mala."

"I know you do, my friend. And what a friend you are to care so deeply for my hurt. But, no. I can't let you assume the burden of our problems. Until there is a solution . . . finalization . . . to the matter, I can't . . . I mustn't . . . you mustn't . . . pursue the . . . or even think . . ."

Tahath heaved a great sigh. "You say *until*. May I then hope that one day, the impediment laid aside, you might consider?"

Mala felt her cheeks flush. There was a long moment of silence while she sought to gather her scattered wits. Then she spoke quietly. "If such release should come, Tahath, there is none to whom . . . for whom . . . I . . . you . . . As we've been bound in special friendship, so might our binding come to . . . to that which is more than friendship."

CHAPTER 6

The hours between her conversation with Tahath on the wall of the synagogue enclosure and the day of his planned trip to Jerusalem held contradictory and troubling thoughts for Mala. It seemed unreal that the incident had taken place at all, and yet she knew it had. It was the enormous, instant difference in her concept of their relationship that made the conversation seem never to have happened. But accepting its reality, Mala experienced wildly fluctuating thoughts and emotions.

Some moments found tears threatening as she sensed the loss of the special friendship she'd known with Tahath. The bond had been much like that between her and Abdon. What a great loss!

The next breath would bring a strange little heart lift as she adjusted her thinking toward considering Tahath not as childhood friend but as prospective husband.

Then her emotional tide would sweep out, leaving bare hopelessness that the situation with her brother could ever be righted enough to allow betrothal.

Next she'd feel almost overwhelming longing to reverse her
response to Tahath; to move forward and surrender herself and her
burden to his care.

Then again she would shake herself free from the troubling
cycle of internal conflict. At that point unease gripped her. Had
that unexpected conversation ruined the special, relaxed spirit of
friendship's bond with Tahath? She alternately dreaded and yearned
for their appointed joint return to Jerusalem.

At last the day came. Waiting outside her house in the early
morning's half light, Mala felt her concern melt away as she heard and
responded to Tahath's hearty hail as he and Belshazzar approached.
She was not only enormously grateful that Tahath's spirit created no
awkwardness; she also recognized it as a tribute to her friend's solid,
selfless character. Mala was glad the dim light concealed her facial
expression. While Tahath added her bundled garments to Belshazzar's
packsaddle, she turned her thoughts to the business of their delivery.

Throughout the days of completing the golden garment, she had
prayed that Lady Terentia might be particularly brief and positive in
receiving it. Since she was now on her way to the dreaded interview
and knew that all of Lady Terentia's responses must be entrusted to
the hands of Jehovah, Mala determinedly concentrated on the day's
more pleasant aspects.

The dawn had been fresh and crisp, reminding Mala that she must
heed Tahath's earlier admonition to purchase a new, warmer cloak.
Perhaps there would be an opportunity to do so in Jerusalem today.
Indeed, she decided, she would make that a definite plan. Though she
would have preferred to construct the aba herself, the commitments
for Lady Diana's household were paramount; her own cloak would
have to be purchased from Jerusalem's marketplace.

"Tahath, if we have time today, could you help me find a new
cloak? I need to buy one, and your knowledge of the marketplace

would save searching the shops and comparing goods. Too, I'm sure the merchants delight in overcharging unwary buyers from outlying areas like Bethphage."

Tahath chuckled low in his throat. "Aye, city merchants are adept at fleecing lambs that wander in from the countryside. I'll be happy to guide you and to keep the shearers away."

At the very moment Tahath expressed cooperation, Belshazzar expressed noncooperation by balking in the middle of the road. They finally prevailed upon the little beast to resume the journey. Tahath directed an exaggerated frown toward the donkey.

"From the outset, Belshazzar protested today's journey more than ever. Age doesn't seem to be improving his beastly disposition." Tahath tweaked Belshazzar's nose as he spoke.

"I think it's not so much a matter of disposition as of art. Belshazzar excels in playing a part. He makes himself the very picture of dejection and overwork!" Mala knew the little donkey to be no more than five years old; she felt his performances resulted from the unusual friendship between him and his master. She smiled, thinking that in this too Tahath was unlike other men she had observed. There were far smaller donkeys carrying far larger loads everywhere about the countryside and with far less show of being burdened. But they belonged to men who only considered their animal to be a necessity and an added responsibility. Tahath and Belshazzar seemed instead to have somehow bridged the diverse worlds of man and beast.

They reached the outskirts of Jerusalem. Rather than struggling against her usual timidity, Mala today found the sights and sounds of the city interesting. She walked through the crowded streets buoyed by her friend's presence. They made their way directly to the marketplace; Tahath left Belshazzar to be unpacked by the owner of the metals shop. But instead of moving on immediately toward the Roman sector, Tahath led Mala to the cloth merchants' stalls.

Passing several, he stopped at a tiny stall whose front was guarded by an equally tiny woman. Swathed entirely in black, the stall's owner squatted on her heels, dark eyes like ripe olives watching the unending stream of passersby. When she saw Tahath, her face fell into an expression halfway between grimace and grin. From the wrinkled lips came a high-pitched, cracking voice. "How goes the world of Bethphage, Metalworker?"

Tahath's easy grin underlined his answer, "Fine and quiet—just as I like it, thank you."

The wizened stall-keeper shook her head. "Your likes need better schooling, I tell you. How much wiser you'd be to come join us here in Jerusalem's marketplace."

At that, Tahath laughed. "You can repeat your advice until the stars fall from the skies, Jedidah; it will never lure me into the dust and noise and bustle of your beloved street."

"Well, then, waste your time and talents out there in your village, if you must—only don't fail to come now and then to let us look at those metal marvels of yours."

At the woman's reference to Tahath's skills, Mala glanced at her friend. She was surprised to see his face redden.

"How you do talk, Jedidah. The pieces I bring to market are no marvels."

"There are marvels of all sorts in this world. My eyes have known the market stalls of Jerusalem for more years than you've been on this earth. My own father was a worker in metals; I grew up in the heat of the forge, and I've watched both the best and the worst plying their skills. Yours is more than skill, Metalworker; it is art."

"Enough of your flattery, my friend. I've not come here for that. Rather, I've come for a cloak—a fine and warm aba for this, my friend

Mala. As you can see, she has coaxed the most possible wear from her present one. I promised to help her find a replacement—fine in quality but affordable in price. I know of no better source than you, Jedidah."

The woman nodded, her little eyes sweeping over Mala. She looked for all the world like a bright-eyed bird in drooping jet feathers. "Though only a villager, you're wise, Metalworker. No one has better cloth merchandise than mine. My time spent here in the marketplace has its reward—superior quality and bargain cost, which I pass on to those who buy from me." So saying, Jedidah rose from her haunches; even at her full height she stood barely to Mala's chin. She led the way past stacked pieces of materials and hanging clothing. Mala was unimpressed with the fabrics, but she recognized quality in the items of clothing. She thought it an odd disparity.

At the very back of the crowded stall Jedidah halted. "Here, Metalworker, are my best cloaks. But, as you see, they hang too high for me to reach. There is, of course, a stool—or you can get them down for your friend yourself. What color do you prefer?" She directed the question to Mala.

It had been so long since Mala had even considered a new garment for herself that she felt hesitant. There were five or six cloaks hanging on pegs. Their colors ranged from black through shades of brown to the color of rich cream. The latter drew her heart, but her practical mind immediately rejected the possibility.

Jedidah's head moved again into its birdlike tilt. "None of the colors appeals to you, is that it?"

Mala flushed in embarrassment. "Oh no. It's not that. The cream-colored one is lovely. But of course that would be impractical."

"So I thought. Well, then, let me show you something I feel will be just right for you." So saying, Jedidah reached to uncover the lower edge of yet another cloak from where it hung behind one of dark brown. Tahath moved to release the cloak from its peg. Lifting it down, he and Jedidah together laid the cloak in Mala's hands. A wide grin split Jedidah's wrinkled visage as she saw the expression which came to the girl's face.

"This is lovely! The dyeing is evenly done, and the color beautiful yet practical. May I try it on?" At Jedidah's affirmative nod, Tahath held the cloak so Mala could slip into it easily. Its weight and length were ideal; the fabric was supple yet tightly woven for warmth.

Watching her, Tahath smiled. "It suits you, Mala."

A small frown creased Mala's forehead. "But are you sure it's not too fine? People in the village mustn't think—"

Tahath quickly interrupted. "People in Bethphage will only think how clever you are to choose exactly the right cloak. All the women will be asking where you found it, and our friend Jedidah here will be besieged with new customers!"

"Exactly what I was thinking, Metalworker. That prospect of further business makes me consider a price that otherwise would be far too little."

"And what is that price, Jedidah?" Mala asked.

With only a brief bargaining period, the price of the cloak was agreed upon. Mala promised to bring payment when they came to collect the cloak following her visit to the Roman sector.

Mala's heart felt light as they made their way out of the marketplace. "Thank you for taking me to Jedidah's stall, Tahath. You were right in saying that her goods excel. Now I must think what to do with my old aba. Perhaps one of Jerusalem's beggars."

"I have a suggestion. There's a small, hairy beggar of Bethphage who would be delighted to inherit your cloak. He has complained lately that the drafts in his stall are bothersome."

Mala laughed. "Aha! Could that beggar's name be Belshazzar? You do well as his spokesman. Hmmmn. Well, I agree to your petition. You may keep this cloak and pass it on to the four-footed beggar with my best wishes."

Mala and Tahath continued on their way to Lady Diana's dwelling. After using the great brass knocker, Tahath handed Mala the bundled clothing items he had been carrying for her; but as he began to step back and out of sight, the aged servant opened the door and, seeing him, insisted that both Mala and Tahath enter. His warmth and friendly insistences were irresistible. Then Mala was taken again into Lady Diana's presence, while the old serving man spirited Tahath away with him into some inner recess of the great house.

Mala delighted to see Lady Diana and her servant girls' excitement over their new garments. Their pleasure, so openly displayed, was payment in itself for the hours of needlework that had gone before. The moments spent with the golden-haired Roman woman and her attendants flew, while Mala marveled at the ease and acceptance she felt in their presence. All too soon she became aware that the hour was growing late; with a guilty start, she brought the visit to a close.

"Lady Diana, forgive me, but I must be on my way. My friend Tahath has business yet of his own here in the city. He has been gracious in escorting me about mine. I would be a poor friend if, in return, I kept him from what he needs to do."

Lady Diana nodded. "Of course. I wouldn't hold you here overlong, though your company is a pleasure. Let's complete our business then. Will this be sufficient payment for the garments you've brought us?"

Mala gasped at the generosity of the amount offered. "Oh, my lady, that's too much! These were simple in design, and the fabric easy to handle."

"You're too modest by far," Diana pressed. "Your work is exquisite, far finer than any I've purchased here in Jerusalem. When working for me, you will receive wages commensurate with your skills. So . . . here." Mala moved forward and hesitantly took the coins from Diana's hand. She could not restrain the tears that came to her eyes.

"Thank you. Oh, thank you."

"And I hope I'm not presumptuous in asking that you return to take another order?"

Mala beamed her pleasure. "I'll be honored to do so, madam. Is there some set time?"

"Let's say a fortnight," Diana responded. "I'm sure that in the days ahead my girls and I will become so fond of these things from your hands that we'll be eager for more."

"Aye, madam. In a fortnight I'll return."

Diana smiled. "Good. We'll look forward to that day. And in the meantime I'll send Zikhi and Mikiah through the shops to search out fabrics. We'll contrive to obtain some that are worthy of your skills."

Mala felt as if her feet were winged as she and Tahath, who rejoined her in the entrance hall, stepped into the street. Sensitive as ever, Tahath caught the tenor of her spirit. "It went well for you with Lady Diana, I take it?"

"Well indeed! No, it went more than well, Tahath. Lady Diana and her serving girls were delighted with their garments and highly complimentary."

"As is appropriate, I must say! Even I, villager as I am, can recognize the quality of your needlework." Tahath spoke emphatically.

"You're a true friend, Tahath, and I owe you much for your encouragement, as well as for your guardianship while I worked on the cloth of gold."

The journey through the streets to Lady Terentia's residence passed quickly as Mala and Tahath carried on lighthearted conversation. When she stood before the great front doors, Mala was surprised to realize that much of her apprehension had vanished. It must surely, she decided, result from the combination of Tahath's presence beside her, Lady Diana's kindness, and her own delight over the new cloak. As her friend drew aside in order to be out of sight when the door opened, Mala stepped confidently over the threshold.

The time with Lady Terentia went far better than ever before. The Roman woman could find no fault with the golden gown. Mala sensed that the woman's mind was racing ahead to some occasion when she would wear the precious fabric, making others envious. As always, however, Lady Terentia was tightfisted in her payment for the gown. Mala had expected nothing else. She nevertheless felt rich both in that she was free of the fabulously expensive fabric and that she was able to make her exit without being given a further commission.

Tahath and Mala returned to the marketplace, where he insisted on purchasing their midday meal. As with the cloth merchant earlier in the day, now too he spoke in easy banter with the seller of food, making it obvious that he was a frequent and well-liked patron. Mala took pleasure in sharing the simple meal with Tahath at the back of the food merchant's stall. When they had finished, she set herself to wander the marketplace alone while Tahath completed his own business. When they met for the return trip home, she carried several parcels containing small household items. A silent prayer of gratitude filled Mala's heart. It had been a long time since she had been able to purchase anything other than utmost necessities. How graciously

Jehovah was dealing with her by allowing so many commissions. She relished the prospect of repaying the several merchants in Bethphage who had sustained her in the weeks immediately following Abdon's departure, trusting her promise of eventual payment. Soon she might even be able to furnish the house comfortably again. In this positive state of mind she made the return trip to Bethphage, and the distance seemed as nothing.

Bidding farewell to Tahath and Belshazzar, Mala entered the quiet darkness of her little house. She stopped abruptly just inside the door. There had been no sound, no sight . . . and yet . . . Her breath caught, and her heart began an uneasy tattoo. She knew, somehow, that she was not alone in the house. "Abdon? Is that you? Are you here?" Her voice sounded like she felt—small and vulnerable.

There was a stirring in the far corner, and a shape darker than the surrounding gloom began to move toward her. Mala instinctively stepped back toward the still-open door. But the voice that came from the dusky interior checked her retreat. "Mistress Mala . . . I'm sorry . . . I didn't mean to startle you . . . It's I, Hodesh . . ."

"Hodesh?" Mala echoed the name with mingled incomprehension and relief. "I did wonder in not seeing you at Lady Terentia's, but what are you—"

"Could you close the door, please? I took great care to come in while no one was about, and I so fear—"

Mala quickly closed the door and disposed of her bundled purchases. Then she moved to light several small oil lamps against evening's gathering darkness. Hodesh stood silently watching until Mala pulled her to a seat near the unlighted brazier. "Now, Hodesh, what does your coming mean? You speak of fear."

"Aye. There is always fear, thanks to the nature of Lady Terentia."

Mala nodded. "I've seen enough on my visits to the household to understand that. So then, you've fled?"

Bleakness looked out from the older woman's eyes. "I've waited long weeks for the opportunity—ever since Lady Terentia told me plainly that she meant to keep me in permanent servitude. I've more than fulfilled my years of service, but . . ."

"Surely then, Roman law is on your side . . . allows you freedom," Mala protested.

"What the Roman law gives and what the Roman Lady Terentia *allows* are totally unlike, I can assure you!" There was a bitter edge to Hodesh's voice.

"So you need my help? I know little of whatever travel arrangements you might need, but perhaps . . ."

Hodesh shook her head. "No, Mistress Mala. My own land holds nothing for me anymore. My family was all killed when our village was invaded years ago. Nor would it be safe for me there. Lady Terentia has powerful connections; her husband is highly placed and important, and together they maintain a network of informants."

Mala frowned. "But why is Lady Terentia so focused upon you? Surely she has any number of slaves."

"The *whys* of Lady Terentia lie beyond explanation. Oh yes, there was my usefulness, and my skill in preparing her favorite foods. But in my case, I believe the matter really comes down to possession. Law or no law, service completed or not, she considers me to be her property. That means exclusive and unending possession."

"But such a situation is ridiculous and unfair!"

Hodesh shrugged. "Nevertheless, it's how things stand. Hence my coming to you. Lady Terentia will not think to look for me here;

I took great care to talk much in past weeks of my yearning to return to my homeland. I didn't use one of her carriages when I delivered the cloth of gold to you; thinking ahead to this day, I hired my own transportation."

"Still, I don't understand your coming here. Bethphage is a small village, and I know of no one who might need—"

"Mistress Mala, I've not only followed my head in planning my escape; I've followed my heart as well. At your very first visit to Lady Terentia's house, I felt a . . . a knitting of my spirit to yours."

"But we—"

Hodesh raised her hand, breaking in upon Mala's attempted protest. "I know. We are very different, you and I. You are a Jew, I a Roman. But we are women—two women in difficult circumstances. You're lonely, are you not?"

Mala nodded in mute assent.

"I, too, am lonely. And alone—utterly alone. There is nowhere else I could think to go." Then the Roman woman drew herself up to as much height as her bulk allowed. "It's not helpless dependency I offer you, but useful service."

"But you're *free* now, Hodesh. You need no longer serve anyone!"

"I've come to think of my freedom as freedom to make a choice. That choice, if you should honor it, would be to serve you."

"But what service could I need?" Mala gestured about her, indicating the house's confined space and its obvious lack of wealth.

"I hear that you've become seamstress for Lady Diana, whom I sent you to see. Moreover, her recommendations have begun flying throughout the Roman quarter of the city; you may soon be flooded with commissions. I've no talent for needlework, but my two hands can relieve yours of duties in house and village that now restrict your time for creative efforts."

As Hodesh spoke, Mala's intended refusal weakened and died. She visualized the suggested arrangement, recognizing the tremendous benefit it would mean. Nor could she resist Hodesh's wholehearted eagerness. When she was able to frame a reply, her voice trembled. "If you will accept a part of my earnings, and if you can assure me that your service will always be your choice rather than obligation, your help will indeed prove a godsend."

Hodesh's face radiated relief. She sank to her knees, took Mala's hand, and held it to her cheek. "Oh, thank you . . ."

Mala was horrified at the older woman's action. "Hodesh, you mustn't kneel to me! All of that is behind you now. Rise. Please." So saying, Mala helped Hodesh to her feet. "It's not homage or servitude that shall bind us together, but mutual care."

Hodesh stood to her feet and wiped away her tears. There was a moment of silence as the two women stood facing each other. Then Mala spoke briskly in order to free the Roman woman from the enormity of her emotion.

"So now, let's attend to practical considerations. Surely the wise thing to do, first of all, is to change your name and appearance. You speak our language well and with little accent, but your name and clothing are foreign. Foreigners attract attention in a place the size of Bethphage. So . . . what would you think of being called? Hmmm . . . *Huldah?*"

The Roman woman had nodded assent at every point in Mala's speech. The draining away of her tension was evident. "Huldah . . ." She spoke the name tentatively.

"She was a prophetess of our people long ago. It is an honored—and a common name—and it begins with the same sound as your real name, making the change easier for both our tongues."

"Then Huldah it is . . . or rather, Huldah I am. But what of clothing? This body certainly can't fit into anything of yours."

Mala hesitated a moment. Then she spoke decisively. "I've kept several things that should fit you." Mala went to a small, leather-strapped chest enclosing a treasure—several garments that had been her mother's. Her hands moved caressingly as she lifted the tunics from the chest and shook out the wrinkles of their years' storage. "Here, Hodesh . . . I mean, Huldah. I believe these will do."

Bethphage's smallness guaranteed its citizens interest and curiosity about any newcomer, and Huldah's sudden arrival brought swift, intense focus. At first Mala was both dismayed and fearful. But Huldah's agile mind, glib tongue, and personal magnetism combined to create sympathy rather than suspicion or censure among the villagers. From the day of her first foray into the little marketplace, Huldah not only put Mala's fears to rest, but she also made her laugh with comic recitals of how she met and dealt with various questioning sessions. Having known Bethphage's residents all her life, Mala marveled at the accurate character judgments Huldah made of each one she met, and how effective she was in winning over even the most reserved of them. Like the leader of one of Rome's famous military units, Huldah set out to conquer the resistant village. She not only breached their defenses, but ended by winning their allegiance as well.

Life for Mala in the little house at Bethphage's edge changed greatly from the moment of Huldah's coming, and the days and weeks that followed passed quickly. Initially there was pain for her both in seeing her mother's clothing worn and in transforming Abdon's sleeping room for Huldah's use. But all of that was offset by the warmth of Huldah's bustling presence.

Talk of Abdon had come naturally as they worked together to clear his room. Mala did not detail her brother's increasingly strange behavior. She only told of his leaving and of her heartache for him. Over the course of days, the older woman simply listened, offering neither comments nor advice. Her sympathetic spirit, however, was comforting.

Although Huldah settled comfortably into Abdon's room, Mala's concern for him did not lessen. In fact, her worry grew greater, because her brother continued his brief nocturnal visits. Abdon's relief that Mala would no longer be alone was overshadowed by his irritation that Huldah was a Roman. The intensity of his reaction was lessened somewhat when Mala gave him the blood red garment she'd completed for Keturah.

At each visit Abdon slipped silently through the door very late at night when Huldah was asleep, her snores rumbling through the little house. Although the whispered conversations between brother and sister revealed nothing of his doings, every visit increased Mala's golden cache. She protested, begging him not only to stop bringing the coins, but to empty the hiding place of all its store. Abdon ignored her pleas; he seemed driven to supply her with the money. He grew increasingly high-strung and distracted, with each visit shorter than the one before.

Because of those tense nighttime visits, Mala more and more valued the normalcy of her daylight hours with Huldah. One morning as the two women worked at their separate tasks, the Roman woman voiced a matter she had obviously spent much time pondering.

"As you've told me something of your life's losses, Mistress Mala, I've heard echoes from my own. Yet in the echo I sense a difference. My years have toughened me—not just on the outside, as with these hands, but also on the inside. In place of womanly softness I've built a warrior woman; one determined not to cringe or cry at life's buffetings; one willing to challenge and defy the gods who sit aloof while they rain hardship upon us. You, however, remain tender. Is it just the difference between youth and age that I see? With passing years will you too curl your empty hands into fists? Or is what I see some distinction between Jewish flesh and Roman flesh?"

Mala responded thoughtfully. "I don't believe the difference is of either age or race. Rather, it seems to me the matter reflects something else." Mala's needle slowed, taking on the measured rate of her contemplation as she continued talking to Huldah. "Were I to see the loss of my parents, Abdon's hardness, and my daily struggles as coming from a distant, cruelly amused god, my responses probably would be like yours. But the holy writings declare that the Lord Jehovah is not such a deity. Rather, He bends in sympathy to us, His creatures. His loving care creates quietness of heart despite life's trials."

Huldah offered nothing in reply. She simply gave her head an uncomprehending shake, gathered up basket and cloak, and left the house for the village marketplace.

As Mala's hands returned to her needlework, her heart was lifted in prayer: "Oh Lord Jehovah, teach me the words to use in speaking to Huldah. Help me to tell her of You in such a way that she can understand. The prophet Jeremiah declares that You urge us to call unto You, that You might show us great and mighty things. I need those great things for Huldah, and I need those mighty things for Abdon."

Mala's prayers for Abdon came from her heart's burden, prayers for Huldah from its gratitude. Insisting that Mala concentrate on her needlework, Huldah moved ceaselessly in, out, and through the dwelling. Each time Mala looked up from sewing, it seemed she saw in the little house some new evidence of industry and inventiveness. The older woman reminded Mala for all the world of the bees buzzing tirelessly about in nearby fields. The likeness was not only in her constant activity, but in its accompanying sound as well, for

Huldah's physical efforts were wrapped in muttered conversation with herself. Mala found the negative, self-admonishing nature of Huldah's commentary amusing. Somehow, for the first time in many weeks she felt a stirring of hope that life might eventually come right again.

Not only did Huldah fit smoothly into Mala's small world and make a niche for herself in the wider life of the village, but she also maintained an active information pipeline from Jerusalem. Mala came to understand that there were numberless tiers of national conscience among the Romans themselves, as well as intricate interweaving between some of those tiers with various individuals among Jewry.

Just as she listened to Huldah's recital of interesting events at Bethphage's village well and market stalls, so too Mala listened to her news from Jerusalem's busy streets. Then one day, in the midst of tapping the informational flow from the village grapevine, came news that brought stabbing anxiety to the girl's heart. Jerusalem was experiencing a plague of robberies. Rather than random incidents, these were carefully planned, meticulously executed attacks by a small band of men. As the robberies escalated, there was increasing unease in the city. The thieves had not only expanded their choice of targets, but the spirit of the gang hardened as its success grew. The robberies more and more included wanton destruction and senseless physical attacks. The battered survivors reported that the group's leader exhibited cold, determined boldness.

Mala's breath caught in her throat as she listened to Huldah's tale. She tried to deny the sudden intuitive chill that swept over her. With great effort, she maintained an air of detached interest. That night as she lay in bed, however, wave after wave of fearful contemplation shook her. Robbers. A small band. A tall, dark-skinned leader so hardened that victims quailed before him. Several others—few, but quick and efficient—who meticulously acted as their leader dictated. Abdon . . . Abdon? Could *he* be one of the mysterious, plundering group ravaging the city? Surely not. Surely her brother's bitterness would never—could never—drive him to such extremes. And yet . . .

what of the gold he brought to her? So much gold . . . Mala shivered in remembrance of the shining coins Abdon poured into her hands each time he made his darkness-shrouded visits.

CHAPTER 7

Aside from the disturbing news of the city robberies, Mala's days were placid as she and Huldah settled into a routine. To her relief, the girl found that she did not have to tell the older woman what to do or how to do it. It was as if the two of them fell into step mentally. Over and over again Mala would find some task completed before she had opportunity to mention it.

From the time of Huldah's arrival and pledge of service, Mala had determined that the Roman woman should have whatever comfort and privacy the little house afforded. To that end, she had avoided going into Huldah's sleeping room. One day, however, after Mala had returned her own roof-dried articles of clothing to their proper place, she carried Huldah's things into her room. As she turned from placing the items on the sleeping mat, she stopped, staring at a small, stepped platform covered with a coarsely woven cloth. Atop the whole sat a squat bit of roughly-shaped, kiln-dried clay.

Puzzled, Mala called, "Huldah, what is this you've arranged here in the corner of your room?"

"That's my house altar, Mistress Mala," Huldah called back.

Mala slowly exited the bedroom. "Your altar? That thing on top is an idol?"

Huldah shook her head. "No. It's my household *god*."

Mala was shocked. She had seen various carved or cast images in the houses of her Roman patrons, and she of course knew Huldah to be a stranger to the Lord Jehovah. But here, suddenly, heathen worship was invading her own house!

Without saying anything further, Mala went to her stool and again took up her sewing. But discovery of the idol had unsettled her heart. As her hands moved in unthinking, accustomed handling of fabric, needle, and thread, she mentally wrestled with the problem that faced her.

The strongest habit her parents had instilled in Mala was adherence to the Torah. They had taught her and Abdon to make Jehovah's written revelation part of daily living. The Law was to be stored in one's memory, but it was also to be consulted and *obeyed*. Mala knew beyond all doubt that Huldah's heathen worship was wrong in the general sense. She knew too, that there was specific wrong in allowing the idol to remain where it was. The fifth book of the Law stated the case clearly:

> "Neither shalt thou bring an abomination into thine house, lest thou be a cursed thing like it: but thou shalt utterly detest it, and thou shalt utterly abhor it; for it is a cursed thing."

Mala felt no confusion about the idol itself; it was consideration of Huldah that caused her heart to question. The Roman woman's coming was unmistakably an expression of Jehovah's loving care. Her presence was a treasure not just in the practical sense of the work removed from Mala's shoulders and the increased earnings made possible, but even more, she had brought the warmth of companionship into the achingly empty rooms. Too, there was

Huldah's already-wounded heart to consider. Surely it would be cruel to renew her suffering by demanding that her familiar religious object be removed. Here in Mala's home the old woman was experiencing the first happiness that had come to her for many years. Further, didn't she, Mala, have the responsibility to represent Jehovah's love to the pagan woman? Harshness with regard to the idol might embitter Huldah, might turn her forever away from recognizing Jehovah as the one true God.

Around and around went Mala's thoughts. For two days and their long, troubled nights she agonized, alternating between determination to demand the idol's removal and fear for Huldah's personal hurt and loss.

At last, after a third night of wakefulness, Mala greeted the dawn with the matter settled in her mind. It was midmorning when she called Huldah from her chores.

"Yes, Mistress?" Mala's heart constricted at the old woman's prompt, bright-faced response. To stop her hands' trembling, she pressed her sewing project hard against her knees.

"Sit down with me here for a time if you will, Huldah." There was a moment of quiet as the Roman woman brought a second stool and seated herself on it. Clearing her throat, Mala plunged into the dreaded encounter. "Huldah, there's something troubling me."

The Roman woman's face fell. "What have I done wrong, Mistress Mala? I've tried . . ."

Mala leaned forward and patted the old woman's knee. "No, no. It's not something—not anything—in which you've failed in your work. You've not just been satisfactory in all of that, but wonderful!" Huldah relaxed slightly from her tensed position, but her brow remained knit in an expression of great concern, and her hands twisted in her lap.

Striving for utterance from a dry throat, Mala went on. "No, it's not your work at all. It's . . . it has to do with . . . with your god—your idol." Mala gestured toward the room that held the offensive object.

"My god? I know it's not a fine image. Had I been able, I would have stolen one of the silver ones from Lady Terentia's, but there was no time. In my haste to escape—"

"Your idol is fine. No, it's not fine, but . . . This has nothing to do with the craftsmanship."

Huldah jumped again into Mala's hesitation. "The placement then? I'll of course be glad to change. I can move the altar to the corner opposite . . ."

Frustrated, Mala shook her head, "No, placement . . . location is not the . . . Huldah, there is but one true God—the God Jehovah. I serve Him. He has declared that we who do so must have no other gods."

"Oh, I wouldn't have you worship my god, Mistress—"

"There is more than that, Huldah. I'm forbidden to allow your god—your idol—to remain here in my house."

Huldah nodded, eager to please. "Outside. I'll put my altar outside, of course, if you so wish . . ."

"Thank you, Huldah." Mala felt great relief, yet she had to continue, making the situation clear. "But even outside it must not be anywhere close to the house here, lest the Lord Jehovah be displeased."

Again the Roman woman's agreement came quickly. "Whatever you say. It really means little to me—so long as now and then I can perform such attentions as to keep my god appeased. If you can keep your Jewish god and I my Roman one happy, perhaps our days shall indeed be blessed from this time forward."

Mala leaned forward, taking both of Huldah's hands in hers. "Oh, Huldah. I want so much for us to have the *same* God! And I pray that just as you now will put your god of clay outside this house, so too you may soon put it outside your life and let the Lord Jehovah come in."

After the heathen idol was removed from the house, life resumed its normal pace and spirit.

Soon after breaking their fast one day, there came a loud, impatient pounding at the door. As always, Mala motioned Huldah into her room before she moved to answer the knock. When she opened the door, she found a neighbor's young son standing before her. His chest was heaving, and as words began to tumble from his mouth, he frequently gasped for breath.

"Mistress Mala . . . quick. Romans . . . two Romans . . . coming this way. They asked . . . where you live . . . Master Tahath told us . . . in such a case one of us children . . . must run . . . warn you . . ."

"Thank you, Jaleph. Thank you! We owe you much. Now you must hurry on home—" The boy disappeared around the corner of the house before Mala could complete her sentence. Closing the door, she called over her shoulder, "Huldah! Did you hear?"

"Aye, Mistress . . ." Appearing in the doorway of her room, Huldah's face was pale and taut with fear. "What shall I . . .?"

Mala was moving quickly through the house, hiding anything that evidenced a woman other than herself being resident. "To Tahath's. Go there. He'll know how to hide you. No, not out the door. They may be close enough to see you go. It will have to be the back window. Here's the stool." Energized by their fear, the two women ran to effect the escape. With surprising agility Huldah climbed onto the stool as Mala steadied it and clambered on out through the window. Mala put the stool back in its accustomed spot, then she swept through Huldah's room, assuring herself there was nothing incriminating there, glanced again over the house as a whole, then settled herself amid her needlework's paraphernalia. Her heart had nearly returned to its normal rate by the time a loud, deliberate knock sounded at the door. Keeping her sewing project in hand, Mala moved to the door and opened it.

"Yes?"

"We've been told that one Mala of Bethphage lives here. Are you she?" The question came from the taller of two Roman young men. Clothed in tunics and togas but with swords hanging from sash belts, the duo was obviously uneasy though trying to camouflage the fact with insolent condescension.

"I am. Is there something I can do for you?" Mala consciously made her tone that of the inferior, timid racial type the two obviously thought her to be.

"Uh . . . Not for us . . . for the Lady Terentia of Jerusalem." The shorter one, this time, responded. As he spoke, he squared his shoulders, as if to add to his physical presence and mental dominance.

Again the taller youth spoke. "The Lady Terentia wants of you two things—first, any word you might have of an escaped slave woman named Hodesh. And second, your visit at once for the sake of a needlework commission."

Steadying herself against the door's edge, Mala bowed her head slightly, assuming a submissive stance. "To the first part, my lords, I answer that I have no word of the slave Lady Terentia seeks. To the second part, although I can't come at once due to prior commissions," she held up a nearly-completed garment for them to see, "I'll come to Lady Terentia as soon as possible—no later than four days hence at the most."

Both the Romans shifted uneasily. It was obvious there was more to their assignment—an additional something that they disliked. "Uh . . ." The shorter man reluctantly inserted his voice into the awkward pause. "It's the further request of Lady Terentia—and the order of her husband—that we search your house for the slave woman Hodesh."

Mala quickly swung the door wide, indicating that they should enter. Instead, the two stood rooted to their spot on the doorstep and let their eyes rove over the small interior exposed to their view. In the quietness of their visual inspection, Mala thanked Jehovah in her heart that two such young and unseasoned men had been sent on Lady Terentia's errand rather than some of the tougher types seen in the streets of Jerusalem.

The Romans left, satisfied by their cursory inspection. Watching their departure, Mala thought she could detect relief in their bearing and pace. Obviously, theirs had been an unpleasant assignment.

With the Romans' terrifying intrusion behind her, Mala had to deal with the sin she'd committed in the encounter. She had lied. Although the falsehood was given to fulfill her responsibility in hospitality and to save Huldah's life, the matter still stood. A lie was a lie. Putting her sewing aside, Mala fell to her knees and whispered a sincere prayer of repentance. Her next sin offering would have a more distinct meaning than in years past. She felt pangs of remorse not only for her sinfulness and the displeasure it caused Jehovah, but also for the innocent creature that must die for her transgression. Yet Jehovah decreed that sin's cleansing was accomplished only through the shedding of blood.

Three days after the Romans appeared at her door, Tahath and Belshazzar once again accompanied Mala into the city. Although they made the journey early in the day, they found the road into Jerusalem crowded and its streets teeming. Just inside the city gate Tahath hailed a passerby.

"Pardon me, but could you tell us the reason for the great crowds today? Is there something special scheduled?"

The man stopped in response to Tahath's question and seemed eager to answer. "To put it accurately, there's nothing special scheduled, but there is a phenomenon rumored to appear today. Obviously, you're not among the many who seek sight of or help from the Nazarene healer."

Tahath and Mala exchanged puzzled glances. "Nazarene healer?" Tahath repeated. "No. We've heard of no such one. Can you tell us more? Who is this person, and . . . ?"

Their informer's brow furrowed slightly. "I share your skepticism; there are many who claim fantastic powers these days. But apparently the Nazarene is not one of them. In fact, I understand that he calls no attention to the miracles he performs—he simply *does* them."

"Miracles? What sort of miracles?" Tahath urged the stranger.

"Miracles of many sorts. The mad . . . the blind . . . the crippled. Many such have been reported healed by this fellow. Nor is it tales from ecstatic imaginers that spread the word of this Nazarene, but solid, sensible citizens who claim they've witnessed healings with their own eyes. The fellow himself seeks no following or fame. He seems, instead, to say—to preach—hard things that drive many away from him. But still great crowds follow him . . . growing daily . . . wherever he goes."

"And the name of this person?" Mala voiced her question shyly.

"Jesus. A plain name and a plain person from all I hear. It's said that he's son to a carpenter in Nazareth. A most unlikely worker of miracles, eh? But be that as it may, it's this Jesus who causes Jerusalem to be bursting her walls today." Chuckling and shaking his head, their informant moved off into the crowd.

Tahath and Mala continued on their way without talking of what they had just heard. For one thing, the noise on all sides in the thronged streets made conversation almost impossible; too, however, the friends were mulling over what they had heard. At last they reached Lady Terentia's house, and Mala steeled herself for the ordeal of yet another meeting with the unpleasant Roman woman. Now Mala knew through Huldah that the characteristic unpleasantness indicated an even darker motivating spirit. She longed for the day when an increased number of commissions would free her from this fearsome patroness.

As Mala entered the Lady Terentia's presence, she immediately sensed a new dimension of coldness. The Roman woman's pale eyes bored into her. Mala's heart formed an urgent petitioning of Jehovah.

"Well, Jewess. You were too busy to respond to my bidding?"

"I am here, madam. I've come as soon as I could finish the projects given to me earlier by others." Mala warmed to realize that her voice conveyed a calm she did not feel. Praise Jehovah for His help!

Terentia twisted impatiently in her chair. She viciously slapped away the hand of a serving girl who reached to straighten a fold of her garment. "What could it be in a base place like your village that forestalls *my* commission here in Jerusalem?"

"Only other commissions from the city, madam."

"Hmmmph. You responded to my needs much more acceptably when Hodesh dealt with you, did you not?"

Mala drew a long, steadying breath. "It's not a matter of the manner in which I receive the commission . . ."

Terentia's eyes narrowed until only a colorless glint shone between the lids. "But you preferred Hodesh, eh? These servant girls tell me that you and she were friendly when you came here to the house."

"Friendly? I try always to be civil—whether to servant or mistress."

"Servants deserve no civility! They should cower in gratitude before the one who allows them to serve."

"I see that indeed all your servants cower."

Terentia's hands gripped the arms of her chair. "But not Hodesh! She should still be here." She pointed a finger down toward her sandaled feet.

"The Roman soldiers you sent told me that she fled your house."

"Fled indeed, leaving not a trace. And you know nothing more than that?"

Mala responded with her own question, "You suspect *me,* Lady Terentia? But why?"

The Roman woman angrily slapped her hands together. The sound was so loud that the two young servant girls flinched. "Of course I suspect you!"

Mala let her arms fall to her sides. "Then you must not desire my further service. Distrust cannot make for pleasant business arrangements." She took a step backward.

"No!" Terentia moved forward onto the edge of her chair. "That's not what I meant. I suspect everyone who had any contact with that wretched Hodesh." Seeing that questions and threatening were working against rather than for her, Lady Terentia moved on to matters of the several garments she wanted Mala to make for her. And at last she indicated an end to the meeting, and Mala exited the house.

Once a safe distance from the Roman dwelling, Mala shared with Tahath the difficulty she'd experienced inside its walls. Tahath frowned as he listened. Then he spoke firmly.

"This must be the last time you come to Lady Terentia's residence. There's too much danger of your making an innocent slip that would reveal Huldah's whereabouts. When you finish this present commission," he gestured to the new bundle Mala carried, "I'll bring the garments to Lady Terentia and let her know that you'll no longer be able to accommodate her."

"But . . . what of her anger? Huldah says it's fierce, and—"

"You and I have no need to fear Lady Terentia; her anger is impotent against us. We are neither Roman nor of the Jewish servant class; she no doubt will fume for a while, but it will be a harmless fuming. And you'll be free from her oppression."

After completing their business, Mala and Tahath headed toward the city gates, aware again of the surging masses of people in the streets everywhere throughout the Jewish section. Amid the jostling crowds, their thoughts returned to what they had heard earlier of the strange man from Nazareth. Too, all around them they heard a word quietly, questioningly, but persistently spoken: *Messiah.*

As they moved on, Mala grew less aware of the crowds themselves and increasingly aware of Tahath's attitude toward them. His usual pleasant expression was missing, and in its place was a deepening scowl. He forged ahead through the teeming streets as if each person who blocked or slowed their way were doing so in a deliberate attempt to offend. At last, after noting with dismay that Tahath even elbowed an elderly man aside, Mala spoke.

"Tahath, what's wrong? I fear we're leaving behind us a great many who nurse bruises as well as hurt feelings from our passage. It's unlike you to scowl and force your way so through the crowds."

Tahath slowed only enough to let Mala come beside him. His eyes blazed as he turned to answer her. "Look at them. They're fools—all fools, these who cluster here in Jerusalem's streets like starving baby birds! How often before have they come, yammering, open-mouthed, begging for wondrous goodness from one or another whom they hope to be our Messiah?"

"We, too, long for Messiah's coming, don't we, Tahath? Why be scornful of these others?"

Her companion's angry tone modulated slightly. "I don't scorn their hearts' hunger. I scorn their mindless rushing from one to another impostor. The failure of so many claimants should slow their eager seeking and mindless acceptance . . . yet just look at them!"

Mala sighed. "The years are long, my friend, since the prophets foretold the coming of our King. In my own heart I hurt more deeply every day for our people. I can't fault others who demonstrate the expectancy we all cherish."

"Humph," Tahath snorted. But his facial expression had softened as Mala spoke, and his stride slowed, both accommodating hers and making allowance for those who shared the streets with them.

Immediately after leaving the city, Tahath and Mala stopped at a wayside inn for their midday meal. Taking their seats at the only vacant table, the two requested food from the serving man, then sat without conversing, comfortable in the silence of friendship. Mala looked about her, ever interested in people and places. They were in a grapevine-covered courtyard; filling the tables around them was a crowd made up mostly of men, though there were a few women and even several children scattered throughout. As she looked about, Mala's attention was drawn to a group of seven or eight men at a nearby table. Their conversation was growing louder by the moment, and it was accompanied by emphatic gestures and reddening faces.

Tahath followed the direction of her gaze as words from the group began to reach them.

". . . the outrage of it! Not only are we bayed by the Roman hounds, but now we're also savaged by wolves among our own kind!"

There was an angry murmur of agreement from the rest of the group.

"Aye, savaged is a good word for it." A new voice joined the one originally raised. "Only savages among us—wolves indeed—would attack and draw blood from our own already-wounded ones!"

The first speaker snorted in disgust. "Who better could know our vulnerability than traitors within our own ranks?"

A third speaker's voice was raised. "But where does this wild pack come from? How has it so flourished?"

The first speaker undertook to answer the query. "No one knows, but some think the outlaws are those whose families were killed by the Romans. Others claim the thieves come from the poorest of the poor, who feel they have nothing to lose. Still others surmise the group is intellectually brilliant—and they've chosen to demonstrate their abilities by outwitting both oppressors and kinsmen."

This last was met by a hubbub of opinions and comments. Then out of the garble came one clear voice—an aged, shrill voice. "What does it matter where thieves come from? What matters is that they are thieves! What matters is that we—we Jews—are their victims! What matters is that their activities are protected—yes, protected, I say— by the fact that we're under Roman rule and thus unable to pursue or punish the offenders!"

"Yes . . ."

"That's true . . ."

"The situation grows worse every day . . ." The babble rose again.

Then once more the aged voice dominated, "The forces of law—both Roman and Jewish—seem unable to have any effect in capturing and punishing the robbers. In fact, questionings and pursuit seem to encourage the thieves, as if they delight in outwitting everyone."

"So what can we do? Where can we turn?"

"Yes, tell us how we can have any hope for relief!" Questions assailed the speaker.

In response, the old spokesman rose to his feet. "Ha. Now we get to the core of the matter. Helpless we may seem, but our strategy and actions must henceforth prove otherwise. What better teachers have we than the thieves themselves?"

"What are you saying, Othniel?"

"Let the thieves teach us? How can they teach, and what?"

"We hoped for the wisdom of age from you—but now this . . . !" The crowd's response temporarily drowned out the old man. Mala and Tahath watched, marveling at his composure in the face of skepticism and scorn. He waited quietly until the uproar had subsided; then he spoke again.

"Whoever they are, whatever their origin, none of us can deny that this thieving band is canny. So, as they've contrived to flaunt their hurt of our people, we must similarly contrive to protect ourselves."

The crowd quieted under the assertion; though grudging, the grouped men granted the old man a hearing.

"The thing we must do is—"

Suddenly the speaker became aware of those at surrounding tables. His eyes traveled around the enclosure, confirming his impression that many were listening to the exchange. "Bend close now and . . ." So saying, the speaker stepped in among his listeners. His gray head disappeared into a sea of dark ones, and only an indistinguishable murmur could be heard from that moment on.

Tahath and Mala finished the light meal, and their silence continued until they had left the city. At last Mala spoke. "How troubles plague our people, Tahath! It's hard to maintain any measure of cheer after being reminded of those troubles."

"Aye, but we mustn't take on the burdens and worries of all whom we overhear. It's enough that each one's shoulders bear his or her own load."

Mala nodded reluctant agreement. "Our worsening burdens— both personal and national—make my heart ache more than ever with longing for the Messiah. Oh that He might come—come and free us from the plaguing oppressions on every side."

CHAPTER 8

The day spent with Tahath in the city sent Mala back to Bethphage with increased awareness of and gratitude for the quietness of her life. That in turn served to give wings to her fingers, and the various commissioned garments took shape quickly. It seemed hardly any time before they were ready to be delivered. It was with relief that Mala entrusted all the garments to Tahath for his next journey to Jerusalem. She was confident that none of the clothing would need to be adjusted; she had made constant measurement checks for accuracy throughout the construction process.

"And," said Tahath in a final attempt to quell her halfhearted offer to accompany him, "as your agent, I'll gladly accept further commissions from Lady Diana but regret that such will be impossible from Lady Terentia."

Mala laughed at Tahath's conspiratorial expression. "Then go, my friend. I fully trust you as agent."

Tahath started to go, carefully holding the bundled garments. But he paused and turned back to Mala. "This morning's start toward the

city is more delayed than usual. The workers at my shop are delayed
in finishing one implement. I'll be hard put to return to the village by
nightfall. Though I'll do my best to hurry, you know how obstinate
my four-footed companion grows when I try to hurry him. If the hour
grows late and I've not returned, send Huldah to find Sethur. I've
arranged with him to begin the night watch whenever I have to be
absent."

"Oh, Tahath, there's no need for you to mount watch each night.
You and your friends have done it too long already. The golden cloth is
gone; only Abdon comes—infrequently and alone. Besides, Huldah is
here now. She's both comfort and confidence."

Tahath shook his head. "The people Abdon has chosen as
companions would consider two women no more intimidating than
one. Nor does the absence of the golden garment cancel the presence
of your hidden gold. Rather than discontinue the night watch, I feel it
would be wise to mount a day watch as well!"

Mala smiled. "You have in effect already done so, haven't you, my
friend? Though guards don't stay close by the house here in daylight
hours as they do in the dark, yet sentries of a sort keep watch. That
was revealed when the boy Jaleph warned us of the two Roman
soldiers."

Tahath blushed his acknowledgement but squared his jaw as
he replied, "And were it not for such sentries, you would've been
surprised by the Romans, and Huldah would have been taken."

"True, Tahath, and we're grateful for your care. But I feel badly
about the inconvenience to you and others."

"Don't. My friends and I aren't burdened by the guard we mount
for your protection. Rather, it adds interest to our lives. We look
forward to that moment when anyone dares to cause trouble for you!
The trouble will, instead, come down upon their own heads."

While inwardly she smiled at Tahath's vehemence, Mala was heartened by the reminder of his caring and its contrast to Abdon's abandonment. She spoke her gratitude warmly. "Thank you, Tahath, for this and all your help."

Tahath blushed again. "Thanks aren't needed. I . . . we . . . feel merely useful in supplying protection for two women who otherwise would be helpless."

There was a moment of awkward silence. Then Tahath shifted the bundled garments with exaggerated care. "Now, I must be on my way. Belshazzar will wonder what has become of me—and, sleepy, he'll be more than ever loath to bear our merchandise into the city. So farewell. I'll bring payment from your Roman patronesses before I return Belshazzar to his stall."

"That's not necessary, Tahath. Keep the payment until tomorrow. In fact, let me come by your shop to collect it. The whole of it must go to others at any rate. How it pleases me to repay those who have helped me! If commissions continue at their present rate, everything I owe will soon be repaid."

On that hopeful note the two friends parted, Tahath hurrying away to add the garments to Belshazzar's load and start toward Jerusalem, and Mala entering the house to begin sewing a garment for one of the village women.

The day passed quietly. Huldah was at times within the house, at other times going about the village on various errands. Toward evening, without moving from the stool on which she worked, Mala had received a thorough update on village happenings.

"There is betrothal, Mistress, between the middle daughter of Machi and the youngest son of Shaphat."

"A fitting match, eh, Huldah? Not only are the families much alike in station, but the ones betrothed themselves have been friends since they were young children. What happy news."

"And the tanner's wife is delivered of yet another son. Late last night, it was. The midwife says that all went well with the birthing."

"As it should. Poor soul. Though sons be blessings indeed, yet their births one upon the heels of another have left Deborah weary beyond her years. She's hardly older than I, yet this marks—what?—the fourth birthing in a short five years?"

"Nay, not fourth but sixth, for there were two babes lost ere they made her middle swell. The midwife feared for this babe too, coming as he did so soon after her most recent loss."

"I'm glad it went well for Deborah. And may this fourth son prove an easy babe by nature, that his mother be not taxed beyond her strength."

"Strength there ever is, somehow, Mistress Mala, for the work of mothering."

"Aye, it does seem so," Mala agreed.

"I wish that you might know that truth beyond mere seeming, Mistress."

Mala paused before she replied. "So much commands my hands and my heart in these days I mustn't allow myself to dream of what might be in some unknown tomorrow, Huldah."

"Then I'll hold dreams enough for both of us, Mistress."

"For both, Huldah? Do you yet desire marriage?"

"No, no. That wasn't my meaning. I meant simply that I'll hold hope for your marrying and bearing children as my own dream and yours as well. As for myself, marriage and childbearing aren't dreams for tomorrow but memory from yesterday."

"Huldah!" Mala exclaimed. "I never thought . . . I didn't know . . ."

"Nor should you have. A slave is a slave—and nothing more."

"But you're far more than a slave to me. From our first meeting there in Lady Terentia's great, cold house . . . But to the point: you've told me very little of your life, Huldah."

"There seemed slight use, Mistress, in talking in detail of my life."

Mala reached out and touched Huldah's hand. "Isn't there the usefulness of understanding to be gained? If only I open the heart's door, our relationship will forever be lopsided due to the closed door of yours."

Huldah responded quickly to the appeal in Mala's voice. "Of course, Mistress, if you're interested in my yesterdays, and if you have the time to hear, I'm glad to speak. I hadn't thought of my silence as a door closed against you."

Mala said no more, but waited patiently for Huldah to continue. The old woman told then of being born into a family in which her father, a prosperous merchant in a village near Rome, purchased Roman citizenship for himself, his wife, and his two daughters. Huldah and her sister married promising young members of the Roman army, and each went with her husband to the post assigned. Huldah's husband became part of the occupational force in Jerusalem. Shortly after their posting in the city, Huldah bore a baby girl, whom she named Patricia. But then came trouble. Huldah's unusual skills in preparing foods agreeable to the Roman palate gave her opportunity to supplement her husband's military pay—but it also brought her to Lady Terentia's attention. Huldah's husband, greatly subordinate to Lady Terentia's, began to be ordered away from Jerusalem to lone outposts, while his wife was more and more requested—or rather demanded—to prepare food for the Roman woman's lavish parties. At last, somehow, Lady Terentia's cold determination had connived not only to circumvent Huldah's Roman citizenship, but also to rid her of both husband and child.

Mala sat open mouthed as the older woman told of her family's disappearance, of her plunge into slavery to Lady Terentia. Every effort to learn of her husband and daughter had been thwarted, and at last she gave up the hope of ever seeing or hearing from them again.

"But, Huldah, how could . . ." Mala's voice trailed off.

Huldah shook her head slowly. "Through many years I tried to discover how my family and my freedom were destroyed, but to no avail. When devastation comes, the one to whom it comes must choose which way to go from that point on. I knew the choice to be one of three: to end my life by my own hand, to live forever afterward in bitterness and seeking revenge, or to toughen and go on to be and to do as best I could manage. I chose the last."

"I'm so sorry, Huldah—sorry for all the awful pain you've known, the treachery . . ."

"But it's past, Mistress. Yesterday need not be lived again, shouldn't be dragged into today. And since coming here the pain has begun to fade. . . . Truly!"

"Would I could make it fade completely. But I know that can never be. To know marriage and motherhood . . . and then to have both torn away . . ."

"I beg you—think no further about it. Had I known my tale would add to the burdens already on your heart, I would never—"

"No, Huldah, I'm glad that you told me. I've allowed my own troubles to deaden me to others' burdens."

Huldah shrugged. "The gods hurl their darts at all. The darts vary in size, and they strike in different places; but every dart is sharp, and each place on the target tender."

Mala's response came quickly. "Although I acknowledge that pain is real, and also, as you say, widely experienced, life's hurts don't come from the hands of cruel gods."

Huldah's mouth set in a firm line. "What of the suffering we see on every side? If gods there be—or fates—or any creatures in a higher realm than ours, what but malignity fuels their treatment of our helpless selves?"

Mala's heart was heavy with the renewed awareness that Huldah—dear, kind, helpful Huldah—was a heathen, a stranger to Jehovah. Life was difficult enough while walking in the knowledge of Jehovah God. How terrible to endure its buffetings without Him! She must do what she could to help Huldah—not just in body, but in soul, as well. "Huldah," she began tentatively, "how did you come to believe in angry gods?"

"What do you mean, Mistress?"

"I mean what's your source of information about your deities?"

"Source of information?" Huldah's puzzlement was evident not only in voice but in the knitting of her eyebrows.

Mala prayed silently for Jehovah to guide her choice of words. "Each of us comes to ideas . . . beliefs . . . through some means or from some source. I don't know the Roman method of religious training; I know only our Jewish way."

Huldah shrugged. "The tales of our gods have been with me for as long as I can remember."

"Tales," Mala repeated. "So it's lore passed down from parent to child?"

"Well . . . yes, basically. But of course there are special days of worship, certain means of appeasement, special celebrations . . ."

"So you learn by . . . by hearing . . . and watching what other people around you say or do?" Mala's probing curiosity was genuine.

"Yes, of course. How else is one to learn of such things?"

"But, Huldah, how did the *first* one of you come to know?"

"There was a time when the gods lived among men, when they mingled with them. The gods, though greater and more powerful than we, nevertheless reflect our human characteristics and habits." Huldah was obviously struggling for expression.

"If these . . . beings . . . are like us in petty attitudes and plaguing actions, how can they at the same time be powerful enough to effect control over us—or to help us?"

"Surely it must be because of their number. With so many gods active all around us, their activity naturally intersects with ours. That's plausible, isn't it?"

"Not really, Huldah. But let's go back to the starting point. You say that your source of information about the gods . . . your basis of belief . . . is word of mouth—one generation telling the next generation, and so forth?"

"I suppose . . ." Huldah's response came reluctantly.

"Think with me further then. How accurate is such a method of transferred knowledge?"

"I miss your point, Mistress."

"Let me give you an example. When there's an interesting occurrence, say, at the eastern edge of Bethphage, what does that event become through repetition by the time it reaches the village's western edge?"

Huldah clearly was pondering the example Mala gave. But she didn't reply.

"The tale *changes* in its transmission, doesn't it?" Mala prodded the older woman. "Perhaps something remains of the original, but there have been so many additions, subtractions, embellishments, and interpretations that the story at its last telling may be barely recognizable as the one that began it all."

"Of course that holds true in everyday happenings, Mistress, but . . ."

"Our *lives* are everyday happenings, Huldah, and our parents' lives were the same . . . and our grandparents and . . ."

"You mean that passing generations would necessarily change the information given at the first."

"Exactly. That would have to happen if word of mouth were the only conveyance of information."

"If that's so . . . I mean if it were so . . . how then would . . . could . . . deity be . . . be conveyed?"

"By written word, Huldah. A god who is truly God would have such majesty, such power, and would in His divinity be so unlike us humans that He would have to *tell* us of Himself. The telling would have to be recorded so that it could be preserved generation after generation."

"By written word?" Huldah repeated the phrase slowly, their deliberate enunciation mirroring the inquiry her mind was making into the words.

"Aye. And there is such a word—a writing from Jehovah. His great Law, our Ten Commandments, was written in stone by His own hand. The history of our people and Jehovah's dealings with them was recorded by men whom He chose and enlightened. We call that the Torah." As they talked, evening's darkness had crept into the room. So intent were the two women on their conversation that they did not notice daylight's end.

Suddenly the door was flung open, and two figures rushed into the room. The smaller of the two closed the door and flattened against it.

"Ho! Why do you sit in darkness, my sister?" The flat, chill voice struck terror to Mala's heart. She reached a restraining hand to Huldah.

"Why do you call me sister? Even in the darkness I know you're not my brother." Mala strove to keep her voice steady.

A throaty laugh answered her. "The term comes easily to one so close to him who is your brother. But . . . yes, there are other terms I'd rather use for you . . ."

"Enough talk! Get on with what we came for." The words came in a woman's voice from the figure still at the door.

"Oh, very well. But mark me, sister of Abdon. Neither words nor our purpose this night will end our interest in you. But for now . . ."

"Light! We must have lights!" Again the woman urged the man toward their purpose.

"You—old woman—see to the lamps!" The man's command to Huldah was harsh.

"Yes . . . yes . . . the lamps." Huldah moved from Mala's side, lit a slender rush from the coals, and went to the nearest lamp, surefooted in the familiar darkness. Flame rose in the lamp, illuminating the four tense figures facing one another.

"Where is Abdon? Why have you come here without him? What is it you want?" Mala's words tumbled over each other. Fear mounted within her. The lamplight accentuated the menace of the intruders— the woman was Keturah, the man Dalan.

"We come without Abdon, because we don't trust Abdon. He disappears too often from our ranks . . . too conveniently after our . . . our collections." The man snarled the words.

"What has that to do with us here? My brother no longer calls this home."

"But he still calls you *sister*, does he not?" Eyes glittering in the lamplight, Dalan advanced toward Mala. "And her he calls *sister*, he cares for . . . and takes care of . . . with gold—*our* gold—doesn't he, *sister* of Abdon?"

Mala had retreated before the advancing figure until the backs of her legs struck the stool on which she'd been sitting. Thrown off-balance, she fell onto the stool. Dalan came close, glowering down at her.

"So now, show us where you've hidden Abdon's golden care of you."

Anger rose in Mala, pushing past her fear. "How dare you enter here. How dare you sneak behind Abdon's back."

"How dare I?" Dalan grabbed Mala's arm, powerful fingers digging into her flesh. "I'll show you how I dare—"

"Let her go!" Huldah rushed forward, brandishing the only thing available—the broom of bundled dry rushes. She brought it down across Dalan's shoulders.

With an angry bellow, the man let go of Mala, whirled, caught Huldah's weapon in one hand and twisted it from her grasp. "Gray hairs should have taught you sense, old woman. But since they didn't, I'll have to do the teaching." He hit Huldah backhand across the face, sending her sprawling on the floor. Then he raised the broom, using the handle clublike, and brought it down with a muffled crack on the old woman's head. Mala buried her face in her hands at the awful sound.

Then again the door crashed open. "Dalan! Keturah! What does this mean?" At Abdon's sudden roar, the intruders froze. Abdon's entrance was a storm of arms and feet, fists and legs. He captured the broom from Dalan, grasped the shaft in both hands and shoved it crosswise against his chest, forcing him to the wall. Then he dropped the broom and smashed Dalan's head soundly against the wall; the man slumped to the floor. Hardly pausing, Abdon leaped over Huldah as she lay on the floor and grabbed Keturah's long, flowing hair, twisting the mass until she cried out in pain. Then he shoved her roughly out the still-open door. Returning to Dalan, he dragged him to his feet. Holding the half-conscious figure with one arm, Abdon turned to his sister.

"Forgive me, Mala. I've been naive in the ways of the people of my new world. But no more. These serpents won't slither away from me again to invade your house."

Mala's tears threatened to choke her in the sudden rush of colliding emotions. "Oh, Abdon, come away from that world. Come back. Back—"

Dragging Dalan toward the door, Abdon cut short his sister's appeal. "No, Mala. It's too late. For I too, have learned to hiss and to strike. But here . . ." As he moved out the door, he tossed her a leather bag heavy with gold. It landed at her feet.

Mala sat staring at the purse as silence replaced the room's mayhem. At length, a moan from the prostrate Huldah brought her back to reality. Mala moved to the door on shaking legs. She closed it gingerly, fearful lest terror and heartbreak reenter.

Another moan of pain from Huldah sent Mala hurrying to her, horrified to have put anything before the old woman's needs. She knelt beside her. "Huldah, can you hear me?"

Huldah's eyes fluttered open. "Mistress, I'm sorry . . . I tried . . ." Her sentence ended in a gasp of pain.

"Hush now, hush. Oh, my dear Huldah, don't speak! What you did was the bravest . . . the kindest . . ."

A shout came from outside. "Ho within! Mala! It's Tahath."

Mala turned toward the door. "Come in, Tahath!" she called.

Tahath entered quickly, his eyes sweeping the scene. He came directly to the spot where Mala sat cradling Huldah's head in her arms. He knelt. "I met Abdon . . . with a fellow he dragged and a woman he drove. He told me to come—that you needed help."

"Oh, yes . . . I . . . we . . . she's hurt, Tahath. That beastly friend of Abdon's . . . Huldah tried to help me."

Tahath slipped his arms beneath the old woman's shoulders, relieving some of the weight from Mala. Huldah groaned.

Mala shook her head. "I'm afraid to move her, Tahath. The blow Dalan gave her was vicious. It may have . . ."

"Aye. We mustn't risk more harm. I'll go for the physician. I won't be long."

"Of course, and do hurry . . ." Mala shifted her legs to a more comfortable position as Tahath lowered the full weight of Huldah's upper body again into her arms.

Without further speech, Tahath raced from the house. Mala's eyes fixed upon the crumpled bag Abdon had tossed toward her as he left. Gold. More of Abdon's wretched gold! Shifting a greater part of Huldah's weight to her left leg, with her right Mala kicked the offending purse across the room into the shadows.

Through a seemingly endless span of time Mala wordlessly petitioned Jehovah for His help. Then the rhythm of Huldah's breathing changed, and her eyes slowly opened. At first they were unseeing, fixed upon the ceiling. Then began a blinking search of the room; finally her eyes focused upward, meeting Mala's watchful gaze.

"Mistress Mala . . . forgive me . . . I tried . . ."

"Again you speak of forgiveness? You're due only *thanks* for trying to protect me!"

"But I failed . . . and now I'm . . . more trouble . . ."

"Hush, Huldah. Please. Save your strength for . . ."

Yet again the door opened. Mala turned her head quickly, and Huldah's body tensed; then both women relaxed at the sound of Tahath's voice.

"The physician is on his way. I ran on ahead, for Dr. Ignatius's great girth restricts him to an amble. What can I do now to help until he arrives?"

Mala nodded toward the clay ewer and bowl across the room. "A wet cloth."

Tahath moved quickly. He crossed the room in a few long strides, poured water from ewer to bowl, snatched a square of cloth from its peg, wet and wrung it out, and came to hand the cloth to Mala. As she placed it gently on Huldah's forehead, the old woman drew in her breath and winced. Simultaneously, a knock sounded at the door.

"Enter, please!" called Mala.

The door swung open, and the village physician entered the room. Ignatius had been physician to all of Bethphage for as long as most of the village inhabitants could remember. While his medical skills and their compassionate use were greatly appreciated, his physical circumference was a source of amazement and jest. His girth had expanded, it was said, with every year of his residence in the village. Whether that judgment were truth or exaggeration, Mala's strained nerves threatened to send her into hysterical giggles as she looked up at the mountainous man looming over her.

"What's this, what's this?" The words wheezed from between open lips as the physician fought to regain his breath. "Tahath could tell me only that someone here had been attacked. What was used to strike her?"

"The broom—the handle of the broom."

"Hmmm. I see. And he used it like a club, I gather?" As he spoke, the immense man moved down onto one knee with great difficulty.

"Yes, like a club. And he struck her full force over the head. The sound was . . . was awful." Mala shuddered in remembrance.

"So it would be." The physician spoke automatically, obviously concentrating on the wounded woman.

Huldah's eyes flew open as the great fingers probed beneath her hair. She gasped, then she squeezed her eyes tightly shut and bit her lip to stifle a cry of pain. Tears appeared through her gray eyelashes. Then her body's sudden limpness signaled loss of consciousness.

"Hmmm . . . mmhm . . . The injury is significant. Had the blow struck lower, say here," he pointed to the base of Huldah's skull, "you would now be without your servant, Mala."

"She's not my servant, Doctor. She's my friend." Mala's rejoinder was instantaneous.

"Oh, but I thought . . . Well, never mind. The point is that she has been spared. As to her recovery . . ."

"Yes?" Mala's voice quavered with concern.

"It is . . . beyond my ability to predict. She is sturdily built, but her age . . ."

"Just tell me how to care for her, Ignatius." Mala's fingers gently smoothed Huldah's hair back from her temples as she listened intently to the physician's instructions that followed. When he had finished, Ignatius heaved himself up from his knees.

"Thank you, Ignatius. I understand what I'm to do. Now if you . . . and Tahath . . . ?" Mala looked her appeal, and Tahath hurried to help. With considerable difficulty the three of them moved Huldah to her room and onto the sleeping mat. Mala was thankful the old woman was spared the pain of their jostling by remaining unconscious. After covering the inert form with a blanket, Mala went quickly to her purse where it hung by its thong on the wall peg beneath her cloak. She shook the coins it contained into her hand, and extended the payment to the enormous physician.

"Ignatius, I trust this will be enough. If not, I can pay you more when—"

"Mala, let me pay the doctor. Please, I . . ." Tahath interjected.

Mala drew herself up. "Absolutely not, Tahath. Huldah has put herself into my care, and I'll pay whatever is needed."

"But had I returned sooner from the city—" Tahath protested.

"Not so. Rather than fault, yours is the credit for yet again helping!"

Following a further brief exchange that included Mala's payment to Ignatius and ended in Tahath's pledge of increased watchfulness, the two men left. Alone in the flickering light of oil lamp and charcoal brazier, Mala dropped her face into her hands and allowed great sobs to rise from the depths of her soul.

CHAPTER 9

For long days Huldah regained consciousness only infrequently. In those wakeful moments Mala urged her to drink, to eat some of the soft, warm meal she kept ready.

Slowly, ever so slowly, Huldah's periods of awareness lengthened. But extending wakefulness also revealed the deeper hurt she had suffered: her thought processes were labored, and she had bouts of alarming confusion. Nor had she escaped long-term physical damage: the left side of her body was weak and palsied.

Caring for the injured woman greatly increased Mala's daily household chores. Commissions dropped off because time available for sewing was so limited. Occasionally Mala thought with yearning of the hidden gold. But she could not bring herself to touch it. Daily strain and solitude filled the little house.

Then all at once a shaft of sunlight pierced the shadows. Gifts of food began to appear at her door. There was some indefinable thing about the food items themselves, the way they had been packeted and the combinations of foods, that made her feel the anonymous offerings came from a man rather than from a woman. When she became further convinced her benefactor was a man and accused Tahath of being that man, he adamantly denied the charge and was intrigued by the mystery. His interest in the food gifts gradually took on other overtones as well.

One afternoon Tahath and Mala sat on the bench outside her house where they frequently conversed. Huldah was napping in her room. Mala had just mentioned to Tahath that she'd found yet more food at her door that morning.

"Hmph. These giftings have become overfrequent, it seems to me." Tahath's tone betrayed irritation.

"But why should they displease you?" Mala asked.

"I'm not displeased, only . . . perhaps . . . suspicious . . ." Tahath shifted uncomfortably on the bench.

"Suspicious! How can such acts of kindness be suspect?"

Tahath examined his work-roughened hands as he answered. "Perhaps there's more behind the gifts than simple kindness, some other motivation."

"But what could possibly move someone—"

"You're a child if you can't discern that, Mala!" Tahath clenched and unclenched his hands. "You feel that the giver is not a woman, but a man. Why, then, *might* a man anonymously become benefactor to you—a woman—a young woman with abilities and beauty?"

Mala felt a burning flush move from her throat all the way to the roots of her hair. "Tahath! You . . . You don't . . . You can't possibly . . ." Her protest sputtered to an end, and the tortured expression Tahath turned upon her caused a catch in her breathing.

"Forgive me, Mala. But my own . . . caring . . . for you makes me, uh . . . hurt with fear that . . ." Tahath's voice was low, his words hesitant.

Now it was Mala whose hands twisted together. "Tahath, you are . . . you've ever been . . . I could never . . . there's no one in the world who . . ."

A great expanse of awkwardness stretched between these two whose lives had been so long and so comfortably intertwined. Then Huldah's voice called from inside, "Mistress! Mistress Mala, where are you?"

——————————

Not many days later, a village woman came to pick up an embroidered sash from Mala. After paying for the item, she pointed to the small basket of figs in the scullery corner. "Is this what the Nameless One left for you yesterday?"

Mala whirled toward her. "What did you say?"

"I just asked if that's the basket the Nameless One was seen leaving at your door. Why? Is something wrong?"

"No, no. I'm sorry to startle you. It's just that . . . uh . . . the food . . . we've never . . . never had any hint . . ." Mala tried to bring order to her whirling thoughts. "You say someone actually saw the Nameless One? Are you sure?"

"It was my sister, Keziah, who saw it, and she's very sure indeed. In fact, realizing that someone saw him leave the food, the Nameless One spoke to her."

Mala's puzzlement was profound. "But that poor, demented creature . . . How could he possibly . . ."

The village woman was surprised at Mala's lack of current information. "You're describing the *old* Nameless One. He's now perhaps more than ever the strangest man to appear here in Bethphage. I wonder that you've not heard of it."

Mala was dumbfounded. "I . . . I have been close bound these past weeks. We know little of anything happening outside these walls. But, please, there must be more . . . some explanation."

"Aye. The story has swept through the village as would a spring storm. The Nameless One's transformation from old to new was the work of Jesus, the Nazarene—that fellow who's as strange as the Nameless One himself!" Thereupon the village woman made her exit, obviously pleased to have enlightened Mala and eager to spread this further interesting note about the food to her village friends.

Mala spent the following hours by physically accomplishing the mundane while her mind probed the mysterious. At last she decided; she must see for herself. The tale she had just heard was fantastic. Only direct, firsthand evidence could prove or disprove it.

The next day, when Huldah settled for her morning nap, Mala laid aside her sewing, donned her cloak, left the little house, and headed toward the village outskirts. When the Nameless One's quarters came into view, Mala felt surging excitement at its changed appearance. Where there had stood an awful hovel, now there was order, cleanliness, and evident care. The wild accumulation of discarded materials and pilfered items had been changed into a home. Mala's steps slowed as she drew nearer to the site. She stopped, timid and unsure as to what she should do next. She longed to see the one living there, but she hesitated to approach the place, lest her action appear unseemly. Just then the door opened, and a man came out. Seeing Mala, he stopped. The two stood for a moment in speechless confrontation.

"I . . . Forgive me if I disturb you, but . . ." Mala finally blurted.

"You don't disturb me," the man answered. "I only wonder at your coming."

"I've been told . . . I felt that I had to see . . ." As she tried to order her thoughts, Mala began to wish she had never come. But the man smiled.

"I don't wonder at your curiosity. As strange as is all this to you in the village, it's far stranger to me. Would you care to hear?"

"Yes. Oh, yes, I would hear! If you really are . . . or were . . . or are changed from . . . the . . . the Nameless One, I . . ."

Again the man smiled. "Don't be embarrassed. I know. I've learned of being called the Nameless One."

"There's little resemblance to what you were, yet at the same time there is a . . . a something that's not recognizable."

"I assure you, I *was* that creature you knew—and tolerated—as the Nameless One. I'll be forever grateful that Bethphage showed forbearance toward me."

Mala shook her head. "He was . . . you were . . . pathetic. Despite your occasional loudness and raging, there was never a feeling of threat."

The man sighed. "For that, I'm glad. The inner tortures I knew could well have driven me to strike out at others. Lest your reputation be blackened, however, let's go somewhere I can tell my tale respectably."

Grateful for the consideration, Mala thanked him, and they agreed to continue their conversation at the synagogue.

Taking different routes, the two arrived at the chosen spot almost simultaneously. Although the few villagers who passed stared curiously at her companion, there was no disapproval in their looks.

As she settled on the shady portion of the stone wall and the Nameless One stood facing her, Mala remembered the earlier time there with Tahath. But she pushed the memory aside, wanting to concentrate on what she was about to hear. Suddenly uneasy, she spoke into the silence that had fallen. "Perhaps I've been overly bold—or rude, even—to seek your story directly. If you would prefer . . ."

"Ah, no. I glory in the opportunity to tell it. I admit, though, that because of what went before, I wished not to return to Bethphage. But I must start at the beginning." He paused briefly.

"My every day was terrible there in that stinking, pitiful heap at the village edge. But on a day even worse than the others the tormenting inner voices drove me out and away. I remember running, running, stumbling, not toward the village, but toward the wilderness. There was a terrible compulsion to put an end to the torture I'd endured so long. Beyond the black, gnawing impulses that drove my aimless flight, I can remember nothing else, until suddenly I found myself standing amid a small group of men. How many there were or what they said, I don't recall. For me only one person was there—one man with whom I stood face to face."

A warm tingling spread through Mala as the man beside her struggled against tears. "And he was?" she whispered.

"Jesus, they called him."

"The healer from Nazareth." Mala confirmed the identity she'd suspected.

The man nodded, and then resumed his tale. "I heard later that Nazareth was his home. Neither name nor native village mattered at that moment of my meeting him. It was as if . . . as if just we two existed—alone—in all of time and space, in all of eternity itself. Indeed, I knew myself to be looking into the very face of eternity! He met my gaze. His look was . . . was of pity, yes, but of so much more. It was a look that plumbed my depths to confront—no, to *command* the awful forces there.'"

"Did he speak to you?" Mala felt she would burst if the speaker didn't move on to complete his wondrous story.

"He said to me, 'Would you be free from your torment?' I fell to my knees, sobbing out my pain, yet unable to form a single word. He touched my head and said, 'Release him, you powers of the dark.' " Again came the emotion-laden pause.

"And then?" Mala breathed, her voice shaking.

"There was a tearing, blistering cataract within me. I knew myself to be falling, but could do nothing to prevent it. That's all I can remember until I opened my eyes, not just to the light of the fading day, but to the light of a dawning life, a new self."

"And the Nazarene? What of him?"

"He stood looking down at me; then he stooped and helped me to my feet. As I once again stood facing him, some great well of certainty opened within me, and I stammered, 'The Messiah! You are the promised Messiah! No other could free my soul as well as my body, as You have done.' "

"And did he deny it?"

"He said only, 'Blessed are your eyes, for you have seen.' Then I begged Him to let me stay . . . to follow Him . . . to help . . . just to be with Him. But He stopped my petitioning, gently but firmly, and told me I was to return to the place from which I had come. My changed self—the miracle He had wrought—was now to proclaim His identity among those of my own village."

"And so you have and are. Everyone in Bethphage surely will speak of you as a living miracle." Having meant for her words to encourage him, Mala was jolted by his vehement response.

"I don't want them to speak of *me*! I want them to hear of the Nazarene. He—and only He—is worthy of attention and wonder."

Mala was quiet, held thrall by what she had heard. The Messiah. Could it be that this Nazarene really was the One sent from God? Was the centuries-long dream of her people at last reality? But how could it be? The Messiah was to be their *king*. This wonderworking man was no king at all, but ordinary—a lowly carpenter's son. She sighed heavily. It was too much to take in; her mind felt it must burst.

Perceptively, Mala's companion went on, "The wonder is immense, I know. How it could even be comprehended apart from a direct, personal experience like mine, I don't know. But perhaps as I demonstrate the new life Jesus gave me, those who see will be drawn not to the changed, but to the *Changer*."

"That is what I feel! The news of your transformation and your anonymous kindness to us . . . for which I've yet to thank you . . . These drew me to this moment's hearing. And hearing, I find myself yearning to learn more."

Mala became aware of the sun's intensifying warmth. She felt a twinge of guilt. "I must go. I've left Huldah overlong. But thank you. Thank you for the gifts of food, and thank you for telling of your amazing newness—and of the Nazarene."

As Mala rose from the wall, her companion shook his head. "Mine are the thanks to be rendered, yet all of life will not be long enough to do so."

Mala started to leave, then halted for one last query. "May I send a friend to you to learn of this Jesus? He needs to hear from you, for he's convinced the Nazarene is like others who have claimed to be Messiah."

"Of course! In fact, I've begun meeting with a few men in the synagogue here. We're studying, comparing the details of Jesus' life with prophecies in the Torah. We'd be glad to have your friend—the metalworker, is he not?—to join us. So farewell. May you, too, find the Messiah!"

Following that climactic moment, Mala found it difficult to take up the daily routine of life. Too, there were ever more frequent interruptions. Huldah's apparent improvement had suddenly reversed, becoming a gradual but definite worsening. Days and nights alike passed with leaden slowness. Mala felt she was being crushed to powder under the combined pressures of sewing, worrying about Abdon, and nursing Huldah. As she sat plying her needle, she often thought how much like a stubborn knot of thread her life had grown.

At Mala's urging, Tahath had begun meeting with the men who were studying the synagogue scrolls. He and the Nameless One, now known as Ezbon, were increasingly in one another's company. Tahath had even persuaded Zichri to hire his new friend, and Ezbon demonstrated a natural talent for metalcraft.

Weeks passed. As Mala was more and more kept house bound, her sphere of existence and Tahath's grew farther apart. She knew that he and others continued their nightly guard duties. But daylight hours allowed only the contact necessary for Tahath to act as her agent as he brought the few incoming sewing commissions and collected outgoing completed projects. She greatly missed the opportunity to enjoy her friend's cheerfulness and encouragement.

One night Mala awakened slowly from deep, exhausted sleep. The darkness was without any hint of lightening in the eastern sky. Why had she waked? She had worked to such a late hour that sleep should have held her captive until cockcrow. Then there came a sound. That must have been what roused her. She held her breath. She must hear it again—identify the sound. There. A strange, rattling gurgle. Huldah!

Mala sprang up and ran into the old woman's room. Her shaking hands made it difficult to pick up the tiny oil lamp she always left burning in the sickroom. At last she and the lamp reached Huldah's sleeping mat. Mala's heart froze at the sight of the old woman's face. Huldah's eyes were staring through half-open lids; her lips were parted, and from one corner of her mouth came a dark trickle. Mala's mind screamed "No!" to the awful certainty that the old woman was dead. But as she stared down into Huldah's ashen face, she saw her eyelids flutter and heard a faint, rasping breath.

Leaving the little lamp, Mala raced about collecting a basin, water, and cloths. Shivering, she paused long enough to shrug into the gown she'd removed such a short time ago. Then she hurried back to her patient. There followed a seeming millennium, throughout which Mala raised Huldah's head and shoulders to ease her breathing, washed away the blood seeping from between her lips, and prayed fervently for Jehovah to preserve the old woman's life. When at last the fingers of dawn reached tentatively into the room, Mala had determined what she would do.

She continued her silent ministrations to the stricken Roman woman until she heard sounds of the village stirring to life. Then she settled Huldah carefully before hurrying to the door to fling it open. A man and boy were passing, heading toward the village center. Mala recognized them as a father and son who lived a short distance farther along the street. "Ho—Sir!" she called out. The two stopped, startled, and turned toward her. "Please. My friend is very ill—dying, perhaps. Could your son run and tell Tahath—Tahath the metalworker?"

"Of course," the man called back. He quickly relieved his son of the several sacks he had been carrying, and the boy raced away. "Is there anything else we can do to help?"

"Oh no, no. But thank you!" The man started on along the street and Mala returned to Huldah. She had scarcely resettled beside the sleeping mat before Tahath rushed in. He had Ezbon with him. The sight of the two men, the sense of their strength and their concern, brought Mala exhausted relief.

Without a word, Tahath helped her up from where she sat at Huldah's side. Ezbon quickly took her place. His big hands were gentle as he pushed the rolled blanket more firmly under the old woman's head.

Tahath led Mala to the bowl and ewer. "Here. Wash." Mala sensed that Tahath's brevity of speech came from tightly-reined emotion.

She did as he bade her, grateful for the water's cool refreshment on her face, neck, and hands. They returned together to Huldah's room. "I'm sorry for my tears, Tahath," she said as they approached the sleeping mat.

"After what you must have endured before Ezbon and I came? The fact that you *only* cried is commendable. And now, I'll go to find Ignatius."

Mala put a hand on his arm. He covered it with his own, and the gesture made Mala's world instantly come right. "No, Tahath. Huldah's need now is beyond any physician's skill. I've seen her steadily decline, watched the uselessness of medical solutions. There's one—and only one—remaining hope for help."

From where he knelt beside Huldah, Ezbon spoke a single word, "Jesus."

"You would take Huldah to the Nazarene?" Tahath asked.

Mala nodded, firm in the resolution she had reached during the past hours at the old woman's side. Tahath said nothing. With gazes locked, the two stood silent for a long moment.

"Well, then, we must get to the task."

CHAPTER 10

Ezbon, Tahath, and Mala worked quickly in preparing for the journey. It seemed no time before the two men drew a light cart up to Mala's door. The boy who had served as messenger in getting Tahath's help had begged to accompany them. Mala padded the cart with blankets. Then the three adults settled Huldah's limp form into the conveyance. They decided upon a specific plan as they readied the stricken woman for the journey. Ezbon and the boy Kadmiel would go ahead to act as scouts. Mala and Tahath, with the cart, would follow. The advance party would determine not only where Jesus was, but also the most direct route by which to reach him.

Only as she stepped back from settling Huldah did Mala realize it was Belshazzar harnessed between the driving shafts. Unlike earlier days, however, the little donkey appeared to be wholly positive in his responses. He moved out readily at Tahath's command. Ezbon and the neighbor boy lingered only long enough to ascertain that the cart and its occupant made a safe start; then they moved quickly ahead along the road leading out of the village.

As Mala left the house and closed the door, she wondered how matters would stand when she returned through that door. They might never find Jesus. Huldah might die from the rigors of the journey. Mala squared her shoulders, shaking off the troubling uncertainties. She managed a small smile as Tahath grinned his encouragement at her.

"Well done, Mala. It makes me happy to see in you the scrappy little girl you were when the three of us . . ." Tahath's voice trailed off as he realized the renewed hurt he might cause Mala by the mention of their childhood circle, of which Abdon had been such a vital part.

Mala lifted her chin. "Much in life is heavy, Tahath, but I'll not be crushed easily! This is a new day, and we move toward hope! The Jesus who transformed Ezbon's entire being surely must have the power to heal Huldah's body."

Tahath nodded. "And Ezbon assured me that he has kept account of the Nazarene's whereabouts. Since we're going early in the day, he's confident Jesus can be found somewhere near Olivet. He's excited to have a part in what we're doing for Huldah. And surely Ezbon is big enough and determined enough to claim a place for us in the crowd, no matter what its size."

"Aye," was all Mala could reply, though she was deeply grateful for the encouragement of Tahath's words. She slowed, dropping away from his side, so she could check on Huldah. The old woman showed no signs of distress at the cart's considerable jostling, and because blood no longer gathered on her lips, she was breathing more easily.

Mala's double focus upon the unknown that lay ahead and the uncertainty within the cart made the journey to Jerusalem's outskirts simply a blur of impressions. She was surprised to see the lad Kadmiel so soon running toward them.

"Ho," the boy called as he approached. Then he reversed direction, falling into step at Belshazzar's head and fighting to catch his breath. "The next turning. Master Ezbon says to take that. Too much crowd straight on. The *back* of Olivet. That's where to go. And we're to wait there. The Nazarene has not yet come from his praying."

"You reached us in good time," Tahath said, stretching across Belshazzar's back to pat the boy's shoulder. "When we take Huldah from the cart to carry her to Jesus, I'll entrust you with the cart's guarding, eh?"

"Oh, yes!" Kadmiel spoke with such quick eagerness that Mala smiled.

After they turned off the main road, they found the way far less crowded and the roadway itself smoother under the cart's wheels. It was only a short distance to their destination. Silver-green trees grew thick along the side of the road. Mala thought how ancient the larger ones must be, knowing the growth of olive trees to be exceeding slow. She sighed, glad that they could stop here, could linger in the shade until the Nazarene should pass. Belshazzar evidently welcomed the shade as she did, for he moved willingly off the track, pulling the entire cart into the shelter of a great gnarled tree.

Now they had only to wait. No, Mala corrected herself. They had only to wait and *pray*.

She and Tahath, along with Kadmiel, had sat resting against the tree trunk only for what seemed moments before they heard voices. Mala rose, using her hand to shield her eyes against the early sun's brightness.

A number of people were emerging from among the olive trees farther along the track, and they began to move toward where the cart with its critical burden waited. Was this the right group, she wondered? Then relief flowed through her as she recognized Ezbon among them. Just as she saw him, he also caught sight of her. He lifted a hand, waving then he ran forward to help get Huldah out of the cart.

In the excitement of the moment, the three easily lifted the unconscious woman, each of the two men holding opposite sides of the blanket on which she lay. Mala steadied the old woman's head against the jostling movements. Kadmiel stood self-importantly holding Belshazzar's halter.

Mala's heart beat in her throat as the Nazarene's party came toward them. She identified Jesus from the focus of his followers' attention upon him rather than from anything distinctive about his person.

Then the two groups came together. For a moment there was silence—one cluster of people with their conversation interrupted; the other, the smaller one around Huldah's quiet form, not knowing what to say.

"You have a need, have you not?" It was the Nazarene himself who spoke. His eyes inquired of Tahath, then came to rest upon Mala. "She is your friend." Mala nodded in silent assent to the statement without wondering why the words had not come, instead, as a question. "What do you seek for her?"

"I . . . she . . ." Mala's mouth felt as if all the dust of Bethphage's streets had settled in it. Slowly, she held out both hands in supplication. "Please. She's dying . . . because she helped me. You are the only one who can save her life."

Jesus looked briefly at Huldah's quiet form, his eyes kind. Then he looked again at Mala. He moved a step closer and lowered his voice. "You do need help, not just for her, but also for another who is dear to you . . . and yes, for yourself, as well."

The Nazarene's face blurred in the tears that came to Mala's eyes. She nodded, a sob catching in her throat.

"I will help. This day your friend will know saving of life. One day—one day soon—your brother, and you, will know something far greater—saving of soul."

Mala felt rooted to the ground. The Nazarene stepped around her, reached out to touch Huldah lightly on the cheek, and then returned to his own group and moved on with them down the dusty track. Ezbon, Tahath, Mala, and Kadmiel silently watched them go.

"What is this place?" Huldah's voice rose querulously, causing all four of them to start. She wriggled and squirmed vigorously in the blanket that suspended her between Ezbon and Tahath. They nearly dropped her. Thereupon followed a spate of mutterings as Huldah struggled to free herself from the enveloping suspension. Once on her feet, her questions came in a flood. "Where have you brought me? And why the blanket sling, I ask you? Mistress Mala, surely you'll answer, though these fellows stand like stumps."

Suddenly Mala burst into laughter, abandoning herself to its wonderful release. First Tahath joined in the near-hysteria, then Ezbon. Even Kadmiel added his high-pitched giggle. Huldah's questions were effectively silenced by the foursome's hilarity, and she stood staring at all of them in uncomprehending amazement.

CHAPTER 11

Life in the little house at Bethphage's edge quickly reverted from the dramatic to the ordinary, and commissions again increased.

Huldah's memory lacked a great chunk of time. In fact she could remember nothing beyond the night of Dalan's attack. The Roman woman's assistance, as valuable as it had been before her wounding, now took on an even greater effectiveness as she worked determinedly to compensate for the time lost and the commissions missed due to her illness.

Mala often remonstrated with Huldah, begging her to allow herself time for ease and enjoyment. But it was evident that Jesus' healing had not just restored her health, but indeed had improved it. The little house fairly vibrated with Huldah's mumblings and mutterings as she carried out her tasks. One day Mala interrupted the buzzing to pose a question that had long been on her heart.

"Huldah, what do you think of the Nazarene—Jesus—who healed you?"

Huldah stopped what she was doing and turned toward Mala. "Of course I've thought much about him. It must be that the gods have bestowed great and unusual power upon him."

Mala shook her head. "No. The power that touched your body touched something far deeper in me. This man has no secondhand empowerment. It's his . . . his very essence."

"I'm sorry, Mistress Mala, but I don't understand."

Mala sighed heavily. "Nor do I, Huldah. Nor do I. I hoped that perhaps the experience of his healing had imparted something more to you—some bit of knowledge beyond my own, which might help me reach a conclusion about his identity."

"A conclusion? We know who he is. A man from Nazareth. Son of a carpenter. An ordinary fellow with extraordinary powers, it seems. His power we can attest. Beyond these things . . ."

Mala sighed again but turned back to the intricate embroidery in her hands. She chided herself for feeling that Huldah had somehow failed her by having only a surface interest in her healer. After all, what more could she expect? She must remember that in everything spiritual Huldah lived in a place apart. If she could be drawn away from her heathen deities to put her trust in Jehovah—that would be enough. Speculations about Jesus of Nazareth, the fantastic possibility of his being the Messiah—those directly affected only Jehovah's people, the Jews—those like Tahath, Ezbon, and Mala. But oh, how she wished . . .

The days ran on pleasantly enough. Mala disciplined herself against worries over Abdon. She wondered, though, at his extended absence. Not since that awful night of his cohorts' attack upon Huldah had he visited. It must be guilt that kept him away—guilt over the fact that the terrifying invasion had come from his friends. Indeed, the anger he had displayed against them as he dragged and drove them from the house had been great. Yet, shouldn't that night have proven to him once and for all that he had cast his lot with a despicable rabble? Couldn't he see? Oh, *wouldn't* he see? Ah, but here she was again, back in the old circles of helpless ponderings.

Mala rose and stretched, trying to ease her burdened mind. Air. She needed fresh air and a walk. These hours of sitting at her sewing tasks were making her body stiff, her mental control weak. "Huldah!"

The Roman woman hurried in from outside. "Yes, Mistress Mala?"

"I'm weary of sitting . . . of sewing. Come with me to the village."

Huldah looked her surprise. "Is that wise, Mistress? If you and I are seen together by anyone connected to Lady Terentia . . ."

"Do you really believe she's still seeking you? Months have passed since you escaped. Certainly she herself would never visit a lowly place like Bethphage. Nor do I imagine she'd even waste sending a thought in this direction since her garments no longer originate here. I remember how scornfully she laughed the day I mentioned that the name means 'house of unripe figs.' "

"Ah, yes, Lady Terentia's scorn is formidable, and it has doubtless increased since the supply of your needlework has ceased. Nevertheless, her contacts are like a great spider's web. Alone in the village I'm unremarkable, but . . ."

"Yes, I see. We must remain on guard against even innocent entrapment. It's terrible to imagine what she might do should she find you now after being thwarted so long. But I do need time outside these walls." Mala reached for her head covering, arranged it over her hair and about her shoulders, then left the house. She moved at a leisurely pace, breathing deeply of the crisp air. She had so long retreated from village life that she found many things new to her: Jozabad's house had been enlarged; there were three small children playing in Bukki's doorway rather than two; Gera's herd of goats was greatly depleted, and the one ram remaining looked bedraggled.

Everywhere she looked there was change. In the marketplace she was surprised to find the old familiar shop of Imnah the candle maker divided into two parts; one half now displayed earthenware, the other half foodstuffs.

She chatted briefly with several merchants; then when she came near the cross street, she turned and headed back for her own house. She moved even more slowly on the return trip, reluctant to end the pleasant solitude of her stroll.

All pleasantness ended abruptly as her house came into sight. The door stood open, and there was a dark spattered trail on the stone step and over the threshold. For a moment Mala could neither move nor think. All of life congealed into the awful picture before her. Then questions began stabbing at her. What did it mean? What *could* it mean? Had Huldah's fears come true? Was the old woman gone— killed, perhaps, and dragged away at Lady Terentia's orders?

Move. She had to move! At last Mala's mind reconnected with her body, and she dashed toward the open doorway, but she stopped again as she reached the step. There was so much blood! She swayed, feeling faint. Then she clamped her jaw, put out a hand to steady herself on the door frame and moved forward, placing her feet carefully to avoid the ugly dark blotches.

Halting just inside the room, she let her eyes adjust from the bright outdoors. The scene that came into focus seemed utterly unreal. In a frightful, twisted sprawl on the floor in front of her lay Abdon, and beyond him, shrinking against the wall with her face drained of color, her eyes wide with terror, was Huldah.

Mala dropped to her knees beside her brother. She could only see half of his face, but it was so battered she clutched at her throat in order to stanch rising nausea. She looked pleadingly toward Huldah. "What? When?"

The Roman woman slowly inched from her place, though she kept her back pressed against the wall and moved crablike toward the doorway of her sleeping room. She stopped then, obviously relieved that she could retreat into it if necessary. Her voice was hoarse when she spoke. "I thought you would never come. He frightened me senseless. I was cleaning. There . . ." She pointed to the far corner where they stored and prepared food. "The door banged open. I thought it broken, the way it crashed against the wall. He stumbled through the door, looking . . . He looked awful—wild and bloody."

"Did he say anything? Anything of what had happened?"

Huldah shook her head. "He stood there swaying . . . looking about . . . speaking your name. Then he . . . he cursed at me. He had just collapsed when you came in."

Mala looked down again at Abdon, and lightheadedness swept over her. She breathed deeply, willing herself to be strong. Abdon was lying face down. He was bleeding so profusely she could not tell where or how badly he was wounded. "Huldah, please. Help me turn him onto his back, then water and cloths—many cloths. I'll do what I can, but we need Tahath . . . and the physician, Ignatius. Go. Please. Hurry. Oh, hurry!"

The two women joined their strength to turn the wounded man onto his back. Then, after depositing water and cloths handy to Mala's reach, Huldah fled, pledging a speedy return.

Mala's stomach churned alarmingly as she began to tend Abdon. Bloody cloths mounted beside the basin, and the water grew crimson. At last she could see the three main sources of his bleeding: his neck, upper arm, and chest—all on the left side of his body. She rolled some of her cloths tightly and forced them hard against the wounds in an attempt to slow the bleeding. She worked silently, too miserable even to murmur, but her heart beat a steady, mournful cry, "Abdon. Oh, Abdon, my brother!"

Mala's knees and back ached from her efforts by the time Tahath came. She looked up at him with mute appeal as he entered, and he knelt beside her. "Here, let me," and he took the cloths from her hands.

"Ignatius? Is he . . . ?"

"Yes. On his way. He wanted Huldah to describe what she knew of the wounds, and he was gathering his supplies."

The following several hours dragged, and Mala repeatedly fought the room's reeling around her as she watched and helped. The physician's concern was evident. At last, however, with Abdon bandaged mummy-like on Mala's bed, Ignatius spoke what encouragement he could, "I've done everything possible." He stopped, seeing Mala's stricken face. He cleared his throat. "Er . . . His body is strong, Mala. And you, I know, are a good caregiver. The next few days are crucial. I'll come regularly, and as you tend him, pray for him. Well, we shall see."

Mala knew nothing of the men's exit. Her world again tightly encircled a sickbed. She pulled a stool to Abdon's side. Then, in her weariness and heartache, she allowed the sea of her emotions to flood out in tears. Only after many long moments did the flood begin to subside. It was then that Abdon startled her by speaking.

"Sparrow. You must stop lest you drown yourself—and me." His voice was weak, but the tone was affectionate and teasing. She sought to dry her tears and leaned forward to look into Abdon's face. Speechless, she simply searched the dear, familiar features.

The next few days are crucial," Abdon mimicked the physician's statement.

"You heard! There will be no *or*, Abdon. The days ahead *shall* move you toward healing! Time, your strong body, Ignatius's skill, and Jehovah's mercy will grant that. Huldah and I, too, will—"

Abdon suddenly jerked as if to sit up; then with a yelp of pain he lay back again. But he scowled up at Mala. "That Roman woman? She's not to touch me!"

"But Abdon, she's my helper . . . my friend. I've told you—and you've seen for yourself—of the difference she has made for me here." Mala was shocked by the vehemence of her brother's outburst.

Abdon spoke through teeth clenched against his pain. "She is *Roman*, Mala. A Roman cur, regardless of how she may lick your hand." Unconsciousness again claimed him, and his body went limp.

Mala held her finger to Abdon's nostrils to be sure he was breathing. Then, knowing there was nothing further to be done for him at the moment, she left the sleeping room. Huldah was in the scullery corner, determinedly washing vegetables. Mala could tell by the droop of her shoulders, however, that the old woman had heard Abdon's outburst. Mala crossed to her and squeezed her arm. "Pay no attention to him, Huldah. His wounds . . ."

"Wounds there are in his body, to be sure, Mistress, but the hatred in his eyes . . . in his voice."

"I'm so sorry, Huldah. He . . . he doesn't know you. It's just the word—the thought—of anything Roman. Come. Let me tell you." Mala drew Huldah out of the house and pulled her down to sit beside her on the little bench. "In talking of my life, I told you only that Abdon and I were orphaned, that our parents died. I didn't tell you how." Mala paused. "Father and Mother were trampled to death—deliberately—by Roman horsemen. Those who saw it say there was no reason. The crowd's unrest, the threatened riot, all had passed. Our parents' killing was apparently simply a lesson, a warning to all of us as subjugated people."

"Oh, Mistress Mala, I'm sorry."

"I . . . I've been able, with Jehovah's help, to put hatred behind me, to think of Romans as individuals—good or bad, as the case may be—just as are Jews. But Abdon . . . The news of our parents' death was brought to me here—at home. Abdon . . . Abdon saw it happen. He watched them—our mother and father—die. He says the Romans . . . he says they *laughed*."

Huldah took Mala's slender hand in one of her well-padded ones. "And you say that your god is not cruel? How else—"

But Mala stopped her. "No. I *know* Jehovah is not cruel. It's men—people, whatever their nationality—who are cruel. The ugly things of humanity spring from the human heart. Jehovah's writings tell of those throughout our own history who have been either good or bad, and the writings make it plain that each person chooses which he or she will be. Jehovah commends and rewards those who choose His way—the good. And He will ultimately bring retribution upon those who choose the bad."

"But to leave you—mere children, and in such a horrible way—without father or mother."

"I can't deny the pain or the loss and loneliness. But long ago the Psalmist penned words of special meaning: 'When my father and my mother forsake me, then the Lord will take me up.' He has done that for Abdon and me. But my brother has somehow closed his eyes to Jehovah's care of us."

Huldah snorted, totally uncomprehending. It was obvious that the two opposing beliefs yet again were at an impasse.

For a fortnight Abdon's wounds kept the household in the grip of uncertainty. He would seem to rally, then sink back into weakness and fever. Mala's exhaustion worsened daily. Huldah of course could not so much as appear in the doorway of the room where he lay, much less take part in his care. So between visits and ministrations by Ignatius, Mala spent her daytime hours tending her brother. Only rarely was she able to sew. Nor did nights give respite. In fact, Abdon seemed to grow worse as darkness fell. It was as if the night itself held a strange oppression for him. Mala slept on a mat beside the sickbed, and as she repeatedly had her sleep broken by his thrashings about or his calls to her, she was convinced that much of Abdon's slow physical healing had to do with his tortured mind. The night terrors that had plagued him throughout their younger years not only continued in his illness, they worsened.

Tahath visited often, but he stayed only briefly each time, wishing to avoid further drain on Abdon and Mala. For the same reason, he spent much of each visit talking with Huldah. Mala, overhearing their conversations, appreciated Tahath's efforts to assure the old woman that Abdon would learn to accept her. Too, he spoke much about the ongoing studies in the Torah that he, Ezbon, and several others were having together.

Whenever Ignatius arrived, Huldah answered his knock, then stepped back and let him make his way to the sickroom. The physician's enormous size seemed to fill any room he entered. Yet his heart and his hands were gentle. At last, he had hopeful news for Mala. "I believe your good care and Jehovah's mercy have blended and enabled Abdon to turn the corner toward healing."

The days that followed bore out the physician's prognosis. Abdon's wounds healed, and his physical strength returned. Mala's gratitude for those changes conflicted with her horrified recognition of her brother's desperately sick soul. Every step upward toward wholeness of body was simultaneously a step downward toward shattered peace.

Huldah and Mala sat in quiet conversation one morning, when Abdon suddenly appeared in the doorway between the rooms. "Well! A sparrow and a crow! Take care, Sparrow. A crow is enemy, not friend."

Stung by Abdon's venomous tone of voice, Huldah's face blanched, and she started to rise abruptly from her place beside Mala.

But the girl put a restraining hand on her arm. "No, Huldah. Stay here. You need not give up your place beside me to his unkindness."

Huldah remained seated, as bidden, but she seemed to shrink into herself under Abdon's glare, and her chin sank to her chest.

"An old, black, ragged crow she is! You should know of crows, Sparrow. We marked them often in our childhood. Marauders they are, remember? They're bully birds—scavenging birds!"

"Abdon, please."

Abdon advanced into the room, coming close to where the two women sat. Assuming his widespread stance, he loomed over them.

"Why do you beg mercy for a crow, Sparrow? Why are you blind to what she is?"

"She is good, and kind, and helpful, and—"

Abdon's face flushed scarlet. "She's none of those things! She deceives you, Mala. A crow is always a crow. A Roman is always a *Roman*!" As he spat out the last word, Abdon gave the stool on which Huldah sat a vicious kick. One of the wooden legs splintered, and the old woman was dumped on the floor.

At that, Abdon burst into taunting laughter. "See the crow now. Fallen from her lofty perch beside you, eh, Sparrow?" He laughed briefly again, then broke into a fit of coughing. As the cough-inspired pain to his wounds made him take a stumbling step backward, Mala rose and went to him. But as she reached out a hand, Abdon slapped it away with his own.

"No," he rasped. "Leave me alone." With that, he retreated, his body hunched against the painful coughing that continued to wrack him.

Mala silently turned back toward Huldah. The old woman was laboring to her feet. She spoke as she dusted herself off. "This must not go on, Mistress Mala."

"But what can I do?"

"Little—if anything. But I can ease the situation, at least somewhat. I'll go elsewhere."

"No, Huldah. This is your home too. It's more your home, really, than it is Abdon's since he chose to pursue another life. That pursuit, obviously, is still very much a part of him. Once his body is fully healed, I fear his refashioned spirit will again lure him away."

"Perhaps. But for now, I must leave. I'll go to ask Leah if I may stay with her. She recently told me that she's not adjusting easily to her husband's death. The empty house is difficult for her to bear."

Mala sighed. "This should not have to be, Huldah. But as in all unpleasantness, we must accept reality. Yet how I dread your leaving!"

"I hope my absence will renew your brother's kindness toward you. Your earlier years, as you've pictured them for me, were very different indeed. Perhaps something of that can be recaptured."

"Oh, I yearn for that. But the more I see of this Abdon, the more I fear the earlier one is lost to me forever."

Huldah moved out with her few belongings that very day. The following morning Mala was quietly breaking the night's fast with fruit and cheese when Abdon appeared, yawning.

"Did you sleep well, Abdon?"

"As well as one can expect, I suppose." He answered glumly.

"Were you in pain through the night?"

"Not of the sort you mean," he snapped.

"What, then? Is there anything I can do to help you?"

Abdon's retort was a roar. "No! No, you cannot help me at all!" And with that he grabbed a cluster of grapes from the small platter on which they lay and stomped out of the room.

Mala sat unmoving, her food forgotten.

Again and again, despite Huldah's absence, Abdon reacted coldly and spoke harshly to Mala's every attempt at sisterly care. As the days passed, he reminded her increasingly of a caged wild animal such as were seen occasionally with traveling entertainment groups. At last the invisible bars against which he struggled were wrenched away. Ben-Oni provided the means of escape.

Abdon's fearsome friend appeared at the house one night long after dark had fallen. Mala was working intermittently on a piece of embroidery. Abdon was restlessly pacing the floor. A loud, sharp, single rap sounded at the door. Startled, Mala made to rise, but Abdon stopped her with a gesture. Eyes alight, he strode eagerly across the room. As he opened the door, Ben-Oni's muscular bulk filled its framework. As he advanced into the room, he gave Abdon a cursory head-to-toe inspection, then his eyes fastened upon Mala. She shrank from the bold stare, dropping her own eyes to the fabric and threads in her hands.

"I regret, Abdon, that your sister does not welcome me more warmly. It has been long since I visited." With an elaborate shrug he moved closer to Abdon, clamping one great hand companionably on his shoulder. Mala ached as she saw Abdon's face radiate pleasure. "It is you, after all, that I come to see, Abdon," Ben-Oni went on. "We of course delighted to receive the word you sent of your recovery, and I came to judge for myself."

Mala's needle poised in midair. Despite his obvious restlessness, Abdon had given no sign of having contacted his companions from the city. She ached to realize that his mind and heart had reached away from her while she was devotedly nursing his battered body.

"Oh, I'm quite well again, Ben-Oni. The days of healing have been long, but my strength is now returned, and I'm eager to escape Bethphage's stifling boundaries."

Mala was stabbed to the heart by Abdon's tone and statement. But she hated the fact that Ben-Oni sensed her hurt. He said, "Oh, no. Don't so disparage this one who has cared for and nursed you back to health. Surely even little Bethphage's bounds are sweetened by the presence of such a lovely attendant. Ah, but to the business for which I'm come. We're eager to have you return to our enterprise, but your full hardihood is a must. The efforts of . . . uh . . . competing forces have considerably increased since you left."

Abdon was eager in his response. "I can help even more from now on! I've thought much, and a number of ideas for improving our various projects have occurred to me."

"Good. I had hoped that might be the case. Well, then, when can we expect your return?"

"There's nothing to hold me here any longer. I'm ready to go with you right now. I've only to get my cloak. Oh. I forgot. The cloak was rather badly . . . disfigured . . . in the event that brought me here. So I must go with you as I am."

Ben-Oni clapped Abdon soundly on the back. "Good. Very good! And once back in the city, we'll see to replacing your cloak—in a manner you'll find more than adequate, I'm sure."

And with that, the two exited the house. Abdon did not give even a glance back to where Mala sat in heart-paralyzing cold.

CHAPTER 12

Mala prayed for her brother more intensely than ever through the weeks following his departure and Huldah's return.

As the weather warmed, Huldah and Mala formed a habit of sitting on the bench outside the door following their evening meal. They enjoyed the relaxation of watching the sun sink to its rest behind the fields outside the village. Then, with the chill of approaching darkness, they would go inside to begin their evening's duties. They were sitting thus, loathing the necessity to leave the fresh air, when Tahath and Belshazzar came into view. The two women watched as Tahath determinedly tugged the donkey's lead rope, urging him onward. Belshazzar's ears drooped. Smiling at the familiar sight, Mala hailed her friend.

"Ho, Tahath! Why are you so hurried? Surely at this late hour Belshazzar's day of service deserves a more leisurely pace on the way home."

As man and donkey drew near, Mala was surprised to see Tahath's face set in a grim expression. She rose and moved toward him. He halted a few feet away, stopping so abruptly that Belshazzar's head knocked him forward another two steps.

"Uh . . . good evening, Mala . . . Huldah. Uh . . ."

"Tahath, what's wrong? You were hurrying to tell me something, weren't you? What is it?"

"Mala, I . . ." Before he would go on, Tahath gently took Mala's arm and guided her back to the bench. Made sluggish by fear, Mala slowly lowered herself onto the seat beside Huldah. Tahath moved a little apart, where he looped Belshazzar's lead rope over a low tree branch. Then he returned to where the two women shared silent, intuitive dread. He squatted in front of Mala and took her hands in his.

"The city was wild today, Mala."

"Wild over the Nazarene? But you've told me that's often true of late. Why should that—"

"No. The wildness was that of relief . . . of victory."

"Victory, Tahath? I've heard of no warfare or riot."

"A . . . an . . . an enemy was captured and imprisoned."

Mala's next question came as a hoarse whisper. "What . . . enemy? Of what sort?"

"The thieves who have so cruelly plundered their own people. Our people."

"And?"

"They were . . . they've been identified."

Mala's unblinking eyes held Tahath's, with all of her inward self gathered in denial against what might come next.

Tahath spoke gently but firmly. "The leader, who called himself Barabbas, is actually . . ."

"Ben-Oni." Mala pronounced the name on a sob.

Tahath nodded assent. "And his cohorts are Dalan . . . and Abdon."

Too stricken for tears, Mala choked, "I knew. Somehow I knew!"

Huldah put her arm around the girl in attempted comfort. "Perhaps it's a mistake, Mistress Mala. Perhaps Abdon was simply in the wrong place when . . ."

Mala shook her head vehemently. "Oh yes, he was in the wrong place, Huldah, but he was there because he's become the wrong person!"

Tahath rose to his feet. "I'm sorry, Mala. So sorry. My heart aches with you and for you."

Mala could not reply.

Tahath's voice reached her as if from a great distance. "We'll go now, Belshazzar and I. I'll come again tomorrow morning, if I may?"

The following days were a living horror. Tahath kept them abreast of news from the city, but all of it was bad. The worry and uncertainties of all that had gone before now seemed shrunken to insignificance. Present reality overwhelmed all. All Mala's internal self was caught in a dark whirlpool, dragging her down toward the fearsome depths of despair.

At the end of a fortnight a wholly unexpected and unwanted visitor arrived in predawn darkness. Because her sleeping room was closer to the door than Huldah's, Mala woke at the first knock and went to answer. As she eased the door partially open, holding a lamp aloft, she recoiled at the sight of the woman standing on the doorstep.

"Mala. That's your name, isn't it?"

"Yes . . . yes. And you're . . ."

"Keturah. Let me in, won't you?"

"But I—"

"I know how . . . unpleasantly . . . you must remember me. But, please. This is different. Very different."

"I'm not . . ."

"Oh. I . . . I see . . ." Keturah's breaking voice and the tears that began to course down her cheeks motivated Mala's decision. She swung the door fully open, watched as Keturah hesitantly entered, then she closed the door and moved with her lamp to the charcoal brazier. The room temperature was warm enough that she needn't light the charcoal. She indicated one of the two stools, and Keturah moved toward it.

"May I take your cloak?"

But the other woman shook her head, and as she lowered herself to the stool she hugged the cloak tightly about her. The two silently studied each other for a moment.

"You know me as Abdon's sister. How . . . how am I to think of you?"

"I wish I could say *as his wife*. But I can't. We do . . . did . . . hope one day to marry, but . . ."

"Then you . . . you love Abdon?"

"I do." The simple sincerity of Keturah's answer sent a tiny shaft of warmth into Mala's heart.

"Is there any hope at all for him?" Mala asked.

"I've tried everything that's come to mind, but I meet only with defeat." Keturah rose from the stool and began to pace. Her next words were bitter. "Ben-Oni wanted to be famous! Now, as Barabbas, it's his fame that makes him—and his partners—prime captives. Romans and Jews alike are exulting."

"So, there's nothing . . ."

"Nothing that has any surety of freeing Abdon."

Mala snatched at the faint possibility she heard in Keturah's statement. "Not surety. But, Keturah, is there somewhere, somehow, a *chance* for his freedom?"

Keturah moved back across the room and sat again on the stool. "The only possible source of hope is so small it's nearly nonexistent."

"Yet it does exist?" urged Mala.

"I can say only that it *seems* to exist." Impassioned suffering shone from Keturah's eyes. It convinced Mala of her genuineness. Although the two women stood on opposite sides of the quicksand into which Abdon had plunged, each yearned for his rescue.

"Tell me," Mala said.

"In my probing I've found one spot at which refusal doesn't come instantly."

"A spot? Of what sort, exactly?" Mala asked.

"An aspiring clerk of law."

"But how?"

"He claims that judgments meted out need not always be in line with what was intended."

"Meaning?"

"He hinted that pressure brought at strategic places can influence a criminal's sentencing."

Mala shook her head doubtfully. "I suppose we all know of that kind of thing being done for important or powerful people. But for the likes of us?"

"He wasn't speaking of important or powerful people. He *was* speaking of us."

"Do you mean he indicated that ordinary people—generally or specifically—could exert pressure?"

"Mala, he was speaking of Abdon's probable sentence—and of us," Keturah's gesture took in the two of them, "and how we might be able to influence the outcome."

"Impossible! Who in authority would ever care what we think, or listen to what we say?"

"No one, of course. But some certainly might care what we *have to offer.*"

"To offer?" Mala repeated the phrase blankly. Then all at once she understood. "You mean money. Money to use as a bribe. Abdon's gold."

Keturah shook her head. "Abdon's gold? No. At this point it's Abdon's life."

"But why do you think I still have the gold, Keturah? I could have done any number of things with it by now."

"I think you have it because Abdon said so. From the very beginning, when he would put aside some after each . . . excursion . . . and each time he would bring the accumulation here to you, he would mock himself for doing so, declaring that you'd never use the gold, because you were suspicious of its source. He said that you live too aware of Jehovah's watchful eye to use dirty gold."

"How I wish my brother had remained aware of Jehovah's watchful eye!" The cry was torn from Mala.

Keturah was silent, her face picturing deep misery.

Steeling herself against her emotions, Mala leaned forward on her stool. "But what might have been and what *is* rarely coincide. So then, to the matter as it stands. From the very first, the gold has seemed blood-tainted. If you can use such ill-gotten money to free a thief, so be it."

Keturah's eyes flashed angrily. "Surely you want him freed? Abdon claimed your love for him was great."

"My love for my brother needs no defense. But human love must be tempered by divine law."

"Then sit here and snivel over what you think to be divine law. But give me the gold!"

Without another word, Mala reached out to test the heat of the charcoal brazier. It was cool, having sat unused since early evening. Using a small iron scoop, she lifted out layers of charcoal and ashes until the flickering light in her clay lamp was reflected from something in the bottom of the brazier.

"There, Keturah. The gold. Take it. All of it."

As she scooped out the heaped-up, long-accumulated coins and put them in a leather bag, Keturah's breath was punctuated with small sobs. "May this . . . be enough . . . oh, may it be enough!"

With little more said, Keturah hid the money under her cloak and went back out into the night.

Just as the brazier was now empty of gold, so too did Mala feel empty of the emotion that had earlier filled her. She was not surprised when Huldah spoke from the doorway of her sleeping room.

"So, Mistress, the wretched gold is gone."

"Aye. And gone for a wretched purpose."

"You trust the woman's truthfulness? She may only want—"

"It really doesn't matter, Huldah," Mala said wearily. "Tainted gold belongs out there, used by or for tainted hands in whatever way they may choose."

Mala moved through the following weeks wrapped in a sense of unreality. Although she recognized the strange numbness of her mental and emotional state, she was thankful for it. Within her was a certainty that she was suspended between two deeps of agony—that which she had already experienced, and some unknown chasm that still lay ahead.

CHAPTER 13

The day began ordinarily enough. Mala and Huldah worked at their separate tasks in silence, except that Huldah's low-voiced mutterings created its usual background accompaniment. By mid-morning Mala began to grow restless. When the restlessness increased rather than lessening, she laid aside the garment on which she'd been trying to concentrate.

"Huldah, I'm going into the village for a while."

"May I go for you, Mistress? I didn't know we needed anything from the marketplace."

"We don't. And thank you for offering to go, but I need both the walk and the fresh air. I'll not be gone long."

As she left the house, Mala breathed deeply of the spring-scented air. She loved this time of year with its signs of freshness and awakening everywhere. She made herself move at a leisurely pace. She watched a bird building its nest; a mother duck leading her ducklings in a paddling parade across a small pond. She stopped to examine a tree, noting that its bare branches were being invaded by tiny, greening leaf knobs.

And so eventually she came into the village proper. The bustle of the small marketplace invigorated her. Then a harsh voice hailed her from one of the merchants' stalls. Recognizing the voice, Mala turned toward its source with dread. When news of Abdon's thievery and of his arrest had swept through Bethphage, reactions were sharply divided. Some extended sympathy and kindness to Mala. Others, however, seized the opportunity either to gossip or to berate her publicly. Azubah the meat-seller was especially vocal and gleeful in doing so.

Dead things—small, pitiful dead things. That was how Mala had always thought of Azubah's merchandise. Carcasses of ducks, rabbits, and chickens hung about the stall. Azubah stood among them, a tall, raw-boned woman whose little eyes and thin lips bespoke her narrow spirit. "Ho! Mala!" She called again.

Only politeness made Mala take a step nearer to the stall. "Good day, Azubah," she said.

The merchant woman's slit mouth rose fractionally at one corner. "Ah, is it a good day for you, indeed?"

"Surely. This lovely spring weather—"

"Lovely weather, eh? Silly you were as a girl, and silly you are as a woman. How can you speak of lovely weather when a storm is about to break over you?"

"You speak in riddles, Azubah. Surely there's no storm . . ."

The meat-seller grinned, exposing over-large, yellow teeth. "Oh, but surely there is! The clouds around your silly head—already dark because of your wretched, thieving brother—are darker still, now that he's to die!"

Mala saw the scene around her pale and shrink. Azubah's voice echoed hollowly. "Ha! You've no answer, eh, Mala? What of your lovely spring day now, eh?"

Forcing words from her desert-dry throat, Mala asked, "Die? You say Abdon is to die?"

"Oooh, yes, die indeed. For once the sentencing has come as fast as it should. Your precious Abdon is to die, along with Barabbas and that other thieving good-for-nothing! Die by crucifixion they will— all three of them!"

Mala whirled away from the death-filled stall and its malicious owner. She stumbled back along the way she'd come such a short, unknowing time ago, deaf to the kind words called out to her by some who had overheard Azubah's attack.

Huldah was sweeping the floor when Mala entered the house. At sight of the younger woman's stricken face, she dropped the broom and rushed to catch Mala in her arms. She half-carried her to the stool at brazier-side, then quickly brought her a cup of water. She knelt before Mala, silently rubbing her hands until the girl's dazed expression faded and her eyes again took on a normal, comprehending focus.

"What is it, Mistress? What happened? What did you see?"

Mala's gaze moved slowly up from Huldah's concerned face to a spot somewhere on the far wall. Her voice was bleak when at last she spoke. "I saw . . . I saw death."

"Death? Was there a fight, Mistress? Someone killed in a brawl?"

Mala shook her head. "Death. Rabbits. And ducks. And chickens. All . . . hanging . . . dead. And then . . . and then . . . Abdon!" A great shiver coursed through Mala's body.

Sorrow and dread built high, impenetrable walls around Mala. Hers was an agony that could not be shared. Although Tahath tried to visit, Mala refused to see him. His own suffering at Abdon's fate made him understand something of her magnified pain.

The scheduled day of crucifixion came with terrible swiftness. Although Huldah begged to accompany her to Jerusalem, Mala forbade it. Strangely, she felt almost relieved the fateful day had come, so great had been her agonies of dread. She wakened from troubled sleep long before dawn, but lay for a time petitioning Jehovah for strength. Then she rose and dressed silently. Everything needed for the day had been laid out, ready, the night before. Although Mala had intended to slip out of the house without waking Huldah, the Roman woman intercepted her as she left her sleeping room, insisting that she break her fast. Mala could only manage to choke down a few bites of bread. Huldah would not let her leave the table until she had drained her cup of goat's milk. She also insisted that Mala take a small bundle of food with her.

"Your walk into the city will use up all strength from this scrap you've eaten. If you're to stay on your feet and to endure what . . . what you must see, midday food will be demanded."

"But Huldah, I don't want—"

"I know you don't. Nor do you think you could possibly swallow anything. But a mortal can't live on air, Mistress. And the greater the strain upon a body, the greater its need for sustenance. Promise me that you'll eat what I'm sending with you."

Although her stomach revolted at the thought of food, Mala promised. She couldn't resist the loving concern that shone from Huldah's eyes.

Mala stepped out of the house into the first faint gleams of the dawning day. The road was so familiar that she needed no lamp to guide her in the brief time before sunrise. A few other dark shapes moved along the road toward the city. Mala fervently wished that her going were as mundane in its purpose as theirs seemed to be.

Although her own mind was benumbed with dread, the city's crowding and hectic activity were unmistakable. She inquired of a kind-faced merchant woman, "Why is there such great hubbub so early in the morning?"

"Ach, this morning and many mornings before as well. You must not have been in the city lately."

"No. I've a friend who serves as agent, both in business and for my Passover offering," Mala replied.

"Passover, of course, always picks up the pace of life. On top of that, we've had other happenings to fill the streets with uproar. But I hear that today will end it all."

"How so—end?"

"Because death's a sure end, eh—both for thievery . . . and blasphemy."

Mala responded from a tight, strained throat. "I know. I've heard of the . . . the thieves. But the other?"

"Oh, that's Jesus—the blasphemer called the Nazarene."

"Jesus! But he's . . . he has been . . . He's performed miracles. He's healed people. He's . . ." Mala protested.

"So they say," acknowledged the woman. "But he has also claimed to be Jehovah himself! Rode into the city like a king, even accepting the worship of the crowds. Can you imagine that?"

Mala could form no words in reply. She simply shook her head, struck dumb by the impact of colliding thoughts, impressions, and emotions.

Misreading Mala's reaction, the woman proceeded. "No, I suppose you can't imagine. The fellow must be mad to proclaim his deity! He's not the first, of course, nor will he be the last. But surely his crucifixion will discourage similar madness—at least for some time."

"But . . . crucified? Jesus is to be crucified? Like a . . . like a criminal? Like a thief?"

Mala's informant laughed. "Not just *like* a thief, but *with* thieves as well. All in all, it's to be quite an event today out on that hill."

Mala swallowed hard. "Yes. Quite. How . . . how can I find the place?"

"What place? You don't mean the execution hill, do you? But why? You don't seem the type." The woman was clearly aghast. "You mustn't go. I've heard descriptions."

"I must I must go. There's someone . . . someone I must see one more time."

"Poor place to meet anyone, I'd say!" the woman snorted. "But if you must, the way is easy to find. According to what I hear, you'll have plenty of company."

As Mala, now supplied with directions, moved on through the streets, she quickly found the merchant woman's prediction true. The streams of people heading for the place of execution grew greater at each cross street. Her feeling of sick dread intensified as she caught snatches of conversation.

"To Golgotha! Hurry! With a crowd this size, it'll be hard to see."

"Filthy thieves! Anything less than crucifixion would be too good for them!"

"Nazareth's madman is coming to his end, eh?"

"So much for miracles. A real miracle worker would make himself disappear rather than face death on a gibbet."

Mala wanted to scream at them to stop their horrible talk—their raucous mockery. She wanted to cover her ears. She wanted to break free of the ghoulish crowd, to run away as far and as fast as her legs could take her. But she did none of those things. Instead, she went on as if she were one tiny bit of driftwood caught in a surging, foaming sea swell of human happenings.

Forever afterwards Mala would marvel at her inability to remember things clearly. Her being, strained to the extreme in its every part, was numb to all but a very few specific moments of experience. Those few moments, however, were not only the culmination of all that had gone before, but also the impetus for all that would follow.

One crystal clear moment was when she learned how terribly justice had been perverted. Abdon and Dalan were to be executed for their crimes. Yet their leader—Ben-Oni—Barabbas, had been freed . . . *freed* in exchange for Jesus of Nazareth! He whose life, work, and self had been only goodness was to die in place of one whose life, work, and self were only evil. Mala knew an indescribable sickness of heart at such insanity.

The place of execution outside the city gates was so tightly packed that Mala at first thought it impossible to move far enough through the crowd to see Abdon. By intense determination and persistent physical maneuvering, however, she eventually won a position immediately behind the line of Roman soldiers surrounding the three crosses. Having reached the spot, Mala allowed herself to look up. Then came the second moment she would remember clearly—the sight of the three men in suspended agony on their separate crosses. The picture burned itself into her mind, and it was so shocking that dark dizziness swept over her. How she wished she could lose consciousness to draw a curtain over the scene. But though her knees gave way beneath her, the crush of the gathered watchers kept her upright and aware. She wanted to close her eyes, but her whole being was magnetically drawn to the cross where her brother hung. Her focus riveted on his tortured face. "Abdon!" Her heart screamed his name, though only a groan escaped her lips. Yet somehow, it was as if he heard. With great effort Abdon lifted his head, and he looked down at Mala. Brother and sister stared at one another for a long moment across the awful, noise-filled distance. Then Abdon closed his eyes, and his head fell forward again.

The physical pain so obviously suffered by the men on their crosses tore at Mala's heart. But the pain of soul she'd seen in her brother's eyes wrenched her even more deeply. In order to endure her heartbreak, she willed herself to look away from Abdon. Her eyes moved first to Dalan. His agony of body was contradicted by the expression of consummate wrath and defiance on his face. Repulsed by the undiminished evil of the man, Mala finally turned her gaze to the figure on the center cross.

As the focus of her attention changed, Mala's mind also came alive to those surrounding her in the crowd. She suddenly realized that their voices, whether angry or mocking, were calling out not to either of the thieves, but to Jesus. Intense hatred moved toward the central cross in waves of sound. The ragged voices issued from faces that were animal-like in their savagery.

As awful as Abdon and Dalan appeared in their cross-bound suffering, Jesus' form on the center gibbet was immeasurably worse. He was, in fact, unrecognizable as the man she'd met so briefly yet so powerfully in Huldah's healing. She tasted bile, and nausea gripped her as she beheld the signs of his terrible torture. "But why?" The question seared her mind like a hot coal. Wasn't crucifixion—this

unspeakably cruel form of execution—sufficient punishment for
even the most heinous of crimes? Yet Jesus was so bloody, so torn
and broken, as to make one wonder how he had survived long enough
to reach the cross. How could human beings wreak cruelty of such
magnitude upon one of their own kind? Although he'd been accused
of blasphemy, hadn't this man's numberless and widespread acts of
goodness counted for some mercy whereby he should have escaped
such awful pre-crucifixion torture?

Mala was jolted from her thoughts by a voice surmounting the
general crowd sounds around her. It came from overhead; it was the
voice of Dalan. He spewed bitter taunts at Jesus. But as she lifted
her hands to cover her ears, Abdon's voice overpowered Dalan's in
rebuke. His words, "we suffer justly for the evil of our deeds, but
this man has done nothing wrong" silenced Dalan's railing; they
also quieted the watching crowd. His proclamation caused lowered
voices and shifting bodies, as if the watchers experienced uneasy self-
questioning. Then her brother's voice sounded again, but it was much
changed. In its tone, Mala heard at last the Abdon of their childhood:
"Lord, . . . remember me . . . when You . . . when You come . . . into
Your kingdom . . ."

A sob tore from Mala's throat. Then she caught and held her
breath as yet a third voice sounded from the crosses. Its authority and
its compassion were profound: "In truth I say to you, this very day you
shall live with Me in paradise."

As Mala's inner world whirled in a giddy vortex, the outer world
was suddenly engulfed in darkness. Fierce wind howled about the
hilltop, and the earth surged beneath her feet. Terrified shrieks and
shouted questions swept the crowd. Mala's own fear was so intense
she felt all creation must be ending, still she could not move from
where she stood.

Above the roar of black wind and heaving ground sounded an
agonized cry, "My God, My God, why have You forsaken Me?"

The darkness held . . . and held . . . and held. Although she could not see those around her, Mala sensed that many were abandoning their places. Gradually all grew quiet in the darkness, and she knew herself to be one of only a few remaining at the execution site. She felt completely isolated, closed in to her own heart's unutterable ponderings.

Another cry pierced the strange, midday blackness. Sounding again from the central cross, it was no longer filled with agony, but with triumph that flooded the hillside. The words engulfed Mala's soul, replacing darkness with ineffable glory. "It is *finished*! Father, into Your hands I give over My spirit."

The words ended, and so did the darkness. The little band of watchers blinked in the sudden brightness, standing as if frozen in the moment. Every eye stared at the central cross, where nail-torn wrists supported a lifeless body.

A new voice sounded—this one close at hand. The words somehow expressed everything that tumbled and surged within her. "Surely this man . . . was the Son of God!" Turning toward the speaker, Mala saw it was the armor-clad commander of the Roman execution contingent.

CHAPTER 14

Again time, its events and its passage, took on a sense of unreality. Mala felt suspended in a gray fog of contradicting sensations: wonderment, grief, exaltation, questioning, and assurance. Then came the final defined and defining moment.

The moment occurred toward the end of Abdon's slow dying. Whether from some human urging toward mercy or simply in order to complete an assignment, the Roman soldiers moved forward to break the legs of both Dalan and Abdon so they could no longer raise themselves to draw breath. Unaware what the soldiers were about to do, Mala not only heard the awful crack, she also saw both men writhe in their increased agony. Then, as she tried to look away, Abdon drew strength from some deep internal source; he raised his head and looked down once more at his sister. In their locked gaze, heart spoke to heart; a great shaft of glorious light penetrated and dispelled Mala's mist of suffering. Through the grime and sweat on his face, Abdon smiled; it was the smile of her gentle, her good, her well-beloved brother. And then he was gone.

How long she continued to stand or why she stayed after life had fled from all three crosses, Mala didn't know. Then came release. A familiar voice spoke softly from behind her.

"Mala?"

She turned. "Tahath!"

Neither one of them moved or spoke for a long moment. They simply stood facing each other while their world of relationship dipped and spun and finally settled onto its lifelong axis. And yet, each knew too, that their world had entered a new universe.

Mala at last found her voice. "How long . . . how long have you been here? I didn't . . . ."

"From the first. You forbade me to be with you, but I had to *come*, nevertheless."

"I . . ." But what she wanted to say could not be said now; perhaps it could never be said. "I just . . . thank you!"

Tahath shrugged. "I'm sorry that I couldn't . . . help . . . somehow."

"No one could. Did you . . . were you close enough to see . . . to hear?"

"Yes."

"Then did you sense . . . do you know?" Mala fumbled.

"Exactly what I see in your eyes, Mala. Much, so much, happened here today—on the crosses and because of the central cross."

"There are no words. I can't express . . ."

"No suitable words can come from us, surely. But all has been expressed by Jehovah Himself, Mala, through His prophet Isaiah:

> And He will destroy in this mountain the face of the covering cast over all people, and the vail that is spread over all nations. He will swallow up death in victory; and the Lord God will wipe away tears from off all faces; and the rebuke of His people shall He take away from off all the earth."

Slowly, silently, Mala and Tahath turned again to look at the central cross, and their hearts paid homage to the form upon it. Surely He was indeed the Son of God. And because of Him life would be forever changed.